3·4·1

Three Tales Told Nine Ways

Stories by:

Christine Ricketts
Nicole DeGennaro
Christopher Rogers

With art by:

Katie Grosskopf
Lauren Feliciano
Justin Carty

3-4-1: Three Tales Told Nine Ways

This book contains works of fiction. All names, characters, places, and events are either products of the authors' imaginations, or are used fictitiously. Any resemblance to actual events, locales, or persons—living or dead—is entirely coincidental.

Copyright Acknowledgements

3-4-1 © 2015 by Christine Ricketts
Just Dessert © 2015 by Christine Ricketts
By Any Other Name © 2015 by Christine Ricketts

Theory of Just Deserts © 2015 by Nicole DeGennaro
Scythe's Fate © 2015 by Nicole DeGennaro
Lighting Options © 2015 by Nicole DeGennaro

The Moon Pulls at Us © 2015 by Christopher Rogers
Good-bye to Nothing © 2015 by Christopher Rogers
Shared Wall © 2015 by Christopher Rogers

3-4-1 Art © 2015 by Katie Grosskopf
Just Dessert Art © 2015 by Katie Grosskopf
By Any Other Name Art © 2015 by Katie Grosskopf

Theory of Just Deserts Art © 2015 by Lauren Feliciano
Scythe's Fate Art © 2015 by Lauren Feliciano
Lightning Options Art © 2015 by Lauren Feliciano

The Moon Pulls at Us Art © 2015 by Justin Carty
Good-bye to Nothing Art © 2015 by Justin Carty
Shared Wall Art © 2015 by Justin Carty

3-4-1: Three Tales Told Nine Ways
Copyright © 2015 by 3-4-1 Publications
ISBN 978-0692551547

Cover design by Katie Grosskopf.

To Mom,
I miss you every single day.
-Christine

To Elodie, Cora, and Charlotte,
Your strength, intelligence, and imagination are all you need.
-Nicole

Table of Contents

About the Authors

Christine Ricketts has been writing for as long as she can remember and boy, are her hands tired. She also enjoys reading, playing video games and theoretical attempts at organization. On rare occasions she will do something involving that so-called "reality" people are always talking about. She doesn't really see the appeal.

Nicole DeGennaro is a human being who exists. Sometimes. When she isn't toiling over the written word, she is often wasting time on the Internet or annoying her cats. She also takes on way too many projects for her own good, but she enjoys all of them. You can learn more about all that at her virtual Batcave: http://nicoledegennaro.wordpress.com/.

With his mediums spanning written word, photography, and voice acting, **Christopher Rogers** is a storyteller above all. A lifetime explorer, his playgrounds have only evolved from his forested backyards in the Hudson Valley to now eleven years in Brooklyn, New York. His preoccupations have been dominated by wanderlust, forging deeper connections, and things ineffable.

About the Artists

Katie Grosskopf is a Brooklyn-based illustrator and blogger whose interests include petting every dog in sight, figuring out public transportation in foreign places, learning about dinosaurs, strategically packing suitcases, and eating pizza. Her work and latest adventures can be found at www.seekatiedraw.com.

Katie provided the art for "3-4-1," "Just Dessert" and "By Any Other Name" as well as the cover art.

Lauren Feliciano provided the art for "Scythe's Fate," "Theory of Just Deserts" and "Lighting Options."

Constantly creating works inspired by New York City, the city he was raised in, **Justin Carty's** paintings use bold brushstrokes and colors to create a sense of motion. This motion he finds inherent within the choreography of the people and architectural forms of the city. He then strives to combine this sense of movement with an emotional realism found within his subjects.

Justin provided the art for "Shared Wall," "Good-bye to Nothing" and "The Moon Pulls at Us."

Acknowledgements

First and foremost we would like to thank the following people that made this collection possible by funding our Kickstarter campaign:

Cullen Gagliardi et al., Matt Pavloff, Lubomira Sieradzka, Kanani Wilson, Barbara A. Waclawek (Aunt), Mason Staugler, Robyn, Tricia Psarreas Murray, David Ricketts, Sinister, Kevan Hannah, Michael Murphy, Ginny Rogers, Christopher Houlihan, Erin & Brian VanDeMar, Sooz Kim, Corey Ptak, Lee A. Forman, DLee, Danni Jerrikko, Chris Kelly, Jordan Schildcrout, Josh Martin, Riley Croghan, Kirk Mueller, Cara & Geoff Sherwood, Kat S., Kevin Walter, Super Dave and Lara Cripe.

You guys are all tremendous and awesome and thanks so much for making this possible.

Christine personally wants to thank Nicole and Christopher for agreeing to be part of this collection and for pretending that they thought it was a great idea. She's glad they're still friends after three years of her hounding them both. She also wants to thank Katie, Lauren and Justin for cranking out some really awesome artwork to accompany the stories. Everything turned out even better than she could have hoped! Finally, she wants to thank her family: Dad, Jess and Tim, because without those weirdos she doesn't know where she'd get these crazy ideas.

Nicole would like to thank her family and friends for always believing in her writing and supporting her love of books; Sangsook Pak for being a willing and enthusiastic first reader and proofreader; the 3-4-1 artists: Katie, Lauren, and Justin, for enhancing the stories with their beautiful illustrations; Chris Rogers for being a great friend and writer, and an all-around inspiring human being; and Christine Ricketts for coming up with the idea for this collection, putting up with Nicole's shenanigans, and being excellent in all other imaginable ways.

Introduction

Whenever I listen to music, I have a habit of changing the words to songs. Not because I've forgotten the lyrics (I actually have a pretty good memory for them; for where I left my wallet or what I was supposed to be doing, not so much) but because sometimes I just think there are much better words that could have been used.

I'm pretty partial to rhyming, so I especially seem to do this when I don't like the rhyme that the original artist came up with.

As I was writing this introduction I tried to think of a specific example to give you, something that would really justify this behavior, but of course I drew a complete blank. (I'm sure it'll happen the next time I turn on the car radio.)

(Wait, no! Totally remembered. So here's an example:

Sittin' there tryin' to look so sweet.
Every word you say is full of deceit.[i]

Which is okay but I always substitute:

Sittin' there tryin' to look so sweet,
But what you said before I'd love to see.)

This habit got me wondering if musicians ever feel the same way about their own songs. Do they ever write a song and then years later think, "You know, I really wish I'd used this word instead of that one? Maybe then that Christine would stop writing me letters about it..."

I know that there are some artists who are always changing the words to their songs in concerts and such but once it's on the radio it's pretty much a done deal right? And even if they could re-record a particular song, what about all of the original recordings? This is the internet age and we all know once something's out on the internet, there's no getting it back. What about all the fans that actually liked the original lyrics? Do you want to risk upsetting them?

I don't write music (which is probably a good thing since I'm 100 percent sure that I'm 150 percent tone deaf; Nicole can personally attest to my lack of musical talent) but it made me wonder if authors might not face a similar situation. Who hasn't written something ten years ago, pulled it out recently and thought, *what the hell was I thinking?*

Now imagine if that were published for millions of people to read. How do you make revisions to something that's already been consumed by the world? George Lucas has been tweaking the original Star Wars trilogy for years and irritating fans with each new iteration. It's kind of like being a chef and making a meal for a customer and then saying, once the customer was finished, that you wanted to change one of the ingredients.

Technically speaking, it's actually pretty easy to make changes nowadays. Now that there's print on demand you don't have to worry about racking up huge bills trying to set up a new print run with a printer. You just update the electronic files and re-upload them to the site of your choosing. But you'll still run into the problem of some people having one version and other people having another. Which story is the real story then?

I was thinking about all of this right at the same time that I was thinking about a particular story that I wanted to write—3-4-1 actually. I conceived the story as something of an homage to one of my favorite stories, which is *The Lady or the Tiger?* I had the plot of the story all laid out in my head but as I was sitting down to write it I started to think about other ways that I might tell the same tale.

(This usually doesn't happen to me. When I write it pretty much only comes through one way with little room for interpretation. I guess my muse is the straightforward type.)

Rather than in the allegorical style of *The Lady or the Tiger?*, I thought about using a more modern setting—something with a hospital, an abandoned construction site, and a war-torn Middle Eastern country.

Then, as I really got into it, I thought about doing an entire collection of stories, all with the same idea but each told in a different way.

Either writer's block or laziness hit me at that point because I couldn't really think of any other stories. I had bits and pieces of ideas but nothing that came together into an actually coherent collection of thoughts or that could, more importantly, fill a hundred pages or so.

And then I finally stumbled over the idea of, what if I had other authors take my story and rewrite it the way they would tell it?

That meant that I would need to find a couple of easily duped . . . *open-minded* writers who were willing to jump into a metaphorical boat with me. I assumed that this part might be tricky—I'm open to feedback and constructive criticism but having someone totally rearrange one of my ideas was a whole other level. I figured other authors would have similar reservations.

Turns out that it's just me. Nicole and Christopher pretty much jumped on board after the first conversation.

Hooray for collaboration!

After that it just seemed like a natural step to bring a couple of artists on board. Who doesn't like a good visual to go along with their words? I thought the artists might enjoy trying something similar with their own works as well.

But I didn't want to be limiting—the real point of collaboration is to help foster creativity. So that's why some stories are strong reflections of each other, like *3-4-1* and *Scythe's Fate,* and others are a bit more abstract, like *The Moon Pulls at Us* and *Lighting Options.*

So as you read, try and see if you can spot the connections between the inspirations for the illustrations as well as the stories themselves.

I hope you enjoy the collection!

---

[i] Hanson. "In the City." *This Time Around.* Mercury Records, 2000. CD

Part I

Choice

/CHois/
noun

An act of selecting or making a decision when faced with two or more possibilities.

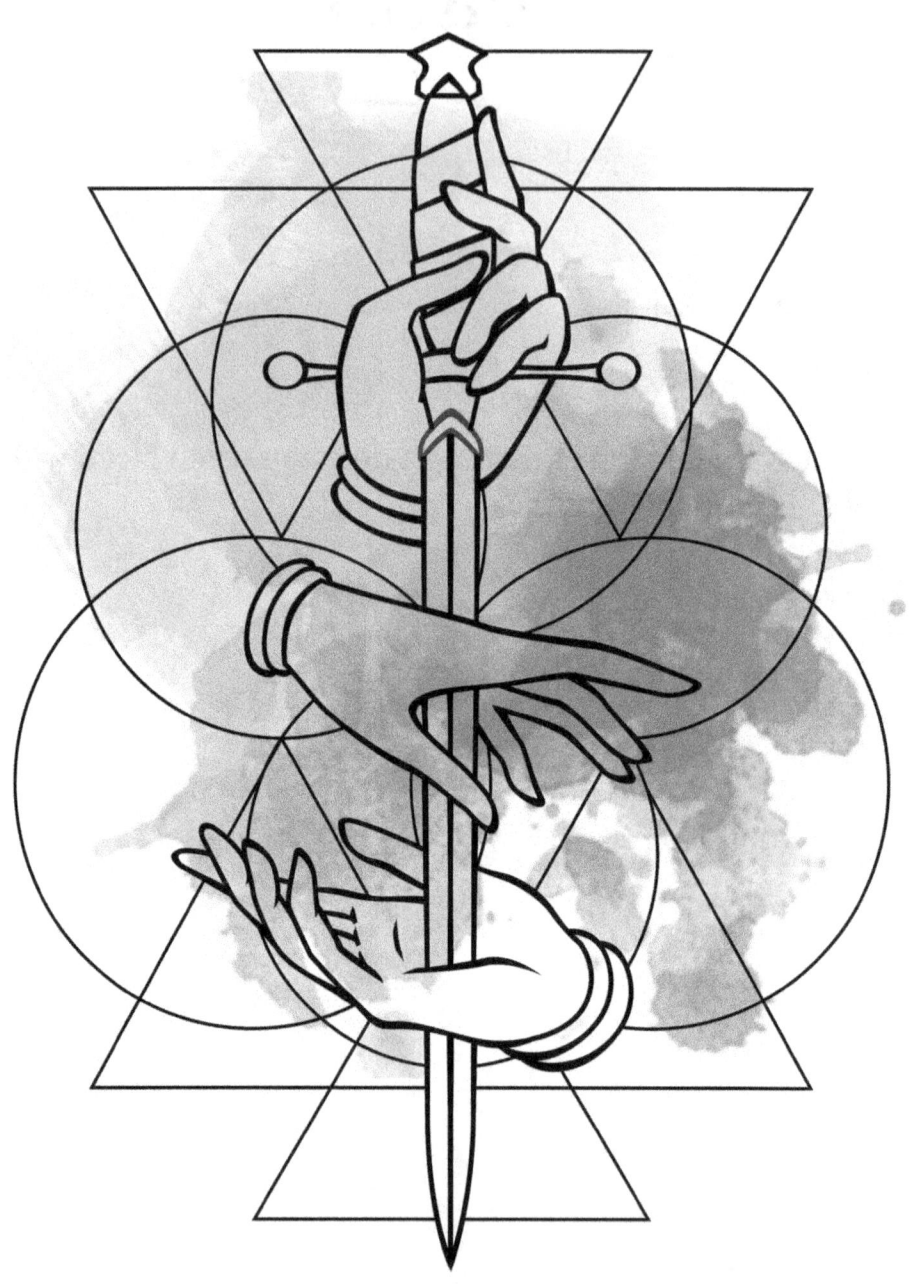

3-4-1

Christine Ricketts

It happened, as it has many times, that there once was a king who ruled over a far-off land. Neither small nor expansive, the kingdom lay on the western edge of a continent. Those who lived beneath the king's banners were happy and those that lived beyond the borders had no objections to their peaceful neighbors. For no king that had held the throne of that kingdom had felt compelled to broaden its reach through war and strife.

Until it happened, as it has many times, that one did. Whereas prior kings had been proud, the new king was vain. Others had been cunning; he was conniving. While his predecessors had watched over the kingdom with devotion, he stared out into the land beyond, desire blooming within.

And it happened, as it has many times, on an unassuming morning, burdened by arms and armor that had not seen the sun in centuries that the army of the king marched.

∂∾∾∂

Opposite the kingdom on the continent's eastern edge, far from the news of violence and war, lay a vast desert. There was neither a kingdom nor any king to rule over it. Only a few dozen villages lay scattered among the shifting sands, home to even fewer villagers. They lived and worked beneath a nearly constant blazing sun as they coaxed what very little they could from the desert's miserly grip.

It was here that there lived a young man of particular note. Tall where the others were bent and broad where others were shriveled by the oppressive heat, yet he wielded his mind with the same ease as he wielded a pickaxe. Both clever and kind, he appeared out of place among the parched dunes. But those within his village, and some beyond, knew that the rest of the world held no allure for the young man. As stingy as the desert could be, it had given him the only thing he wished: his beloved.

The daughter of the village elder, the beauty of her countenance was eclipsed only by that of her spirit. She was much loved by all who knew her, but none as much as the young man. And the level of fidelity that he bestowed upon her was returned with equal fervor. No matter how scorching the heat or how tiring the work the sight of the two youths together brought a smile to all who bore witness.

One day, without warning, the daughter grew very ill. The village healer came quickly but could not deduce the cause of her sickness. Nor did any of the herbs in his possession bring any relief. The elder dispatched messages to other villages and healers from all across the desert came. But none knew the cause of her illness and each shook his or her head when asked what could be done. Day and night the young man knelt beside his beloved, his eyes never leaving her face as he listened to the words of bafflement that fell from the lips of each healer that came and went.

&roc&

The king's army fell upon the cities just beyond the kingdom's walls, crushing all but the cries of war that echoed in its wake.

&roc&

It was late in the witching hour when a doctor from outside the desert entered the elder's tent. Like the others before him he examined the daughter closely; measured the beat of her heart, the temperature of her skin. When he had finished, the same confusion was etched upon his brow. Only this time when he turned and shook his head he murmured *that it would take all three of a* djinn's *wishes to save that girl.* And with nothing more offered, he exited as quietly as he had entered.

The words echoed in the young man's head for hours after the doctor had left. When morning came, the elder found him seated just as he had been the night before and the night before that and the night before that. Accustomed to his silent vigil, the elder was surprised when the young man lifted his eyes from the face of his beloved and asked what he knew of the *djinn*. Perplexed, but ever willing to share knowledge, the elder spoke of god-like beings with eyes of blue fire said to grant three wishes to those lucky enough to find one.

As the words left his lips, the elder was filled with sorrowed understanding. *Such things*, he told the young man gently, *lived only in legends, far beyond reach*. The young man bowed his head politely and fell silent, his gaze returning to its post. His battered heart made even heavier for the youth that shared his grief, the elder turned away and missed the grim determination that settled across the young man's face.

ॐ

Saddened by the illness of one they had so admired, the other villagers all took turns visiting the elder's tent; some bore gifts, others offered to run errands, all gave words of hope and encouragement. Each shook his or her head when asked how or where one could find a *djinn*. *Such things*, they all said with sympathy in their eyes, *lived only in legend*. The young man nodded, thanked them, and waited for the next to arrive.

Until, at last, there were none who had not been asked and none who had not answered. And when the final villager had departed the elder's tent and twilight had once more descended, the young man turned his thoughts inward. Even the wildest story, he reasoned to himself, contained some grain of truth. What was a legend but a story older than most?

The next morning when the elder awoke and went to check on his daughter, he found the small stool beside her cot empty, save for a scrap of parchment. Leaning down, the elder read the words scrawled out in the young man's flowing script.

So long as such things live somewhere, I will find one.

ॐ

One by one, whether through intimidation or bloodshed, the cities of the continent submitted to the might of the king's army. Rumors of violence became scars of battle as the arm of the king reached farther and farther east.

ॐ

With only a small satchel of supplies, the young man cast himself out into the desert, heedless of the stinging winds and burning sun. He traveled for a long time, stopping only to eat, drink or ask any he came across if they knew where he might find one of the *djinn*. Every person he met shook his or her head and said *such things lived only in legends*. And did he not know of the army that drew closer every day? Better to take his beloved and flee before it was too late.

But the young man persisted, brushing aside the news of war. What king could desire a land that would ever take more than it gave, he reasoned to himself.

It was many weeks into his journey when the young man came upon the ancient beggar sitting at a crossroads just outside a small village so similar to his own.

ॐ∞ᄋ

When he drew close enough, the young man could see that the beggar's eyes were closed but he was not asleep. His head, topped with long, snowy-white hair that stood stark against his weathered skin, bobbed and his dry, cracked lips moved ever so slightly as quietly murmured words fell between them. *3, 4, 1. 3, 4, 1*, the beggar mumbled. A small wooden bowl sat before him, a single coin set within. *3, 4, 1.*

The beggar paused his prayer at the sound of a second coin rattling in his bowl but did not open his eyes. *There is more where that came from if you know where I may find one of the* djinn, the young man promised.

Without opening his eyes, the old beggar tilted his head in the direction of the young man's voice and his lips fell open once more. *3, 4, 1. 3, 4, 1.*

Disappointed, the young man turned to walk away. But before he had taken his first step, he reached into his purse and dropped a second coin in the beggar's bowl. Once more the beggar's prayer stopped and whispered words trickled out along the desert wind.

ॐ∞ᄋ

Following the old beggar's directions, the young man traveled north for three days. Each hour was hotter than the last and not even the night brought any relief. On the morning of the third day, as the sun and temperature climbed, he came upon a white tree, its bark peeling off in sickly waves. Not far beyond, cut into the base of a crag of rock, was the opening of a cave, pitch black against the blinding light of the sun.

ॐ∞ᄋ

Stumbling, the young man pushed forward, the chill of darkness sweeping over his sun-stroked skin. The air within the cave was cool, almost cold, and moist compared to the arid desert. And the floor, though hard and firm rather than soft and shifting, felt uneven, as if tilted. From his satchel he procured a small waterskin and, lifting it to his lips, drank deeply. But though the tepid water eased his parched throat the feeling of imbalance stubbornly remained.

He stood a long while just within the cave's mouth, waiting for his eyes to adjust to the blackness. For the first time in his journey, he felt trembles of fear in his legs as he slowly began to put one foot in front of the other.

It was difficult to say just how long he walked before the darkness was suddenly swept aside by a wave of bluish light. As he turned to follow its sweeping pass through the air, he found himself face to face with a tall figure. Swathed in clothes of midnight that bled into the shadows surrounding them, its pale skin appeared almost grey. The blue light hovered over its shoulder and danced within its irises like tiny flames. No, the young man corrected silently, its eyes *were* blue flames.

His heart beginning to thrum with nerves that had up until this point been unfelt, the young man asked if it were a *djinn* and if it would grant him three wishes. The figure smiled faintly and answered the first question without speaking and the second with a question of its own. *What would he offer in return*? The young man gave a puzzled look. *In return for what*, he wanted to know.

Now the *djinn* laughed. *Your kind*, it mused, *always so certain that something can be gotten for nothing*. It would not grant the young man three wishes—it would not grant him one wish without payment.

Frowning, the young man reached into his purse for coin but the *djinn* merely laughed again, soft and high. *The price of magic was far dearer than any bit of shiny metal*, it explained.

Then what did it want, the young man asked, growing annoyed with the creature's laughter. The *djinn* lifted its arm and held out a thin object toward him that the dim glow failed to illuminate. Stepping closer, the young man reached out for it, his fingers curling around smooth leather.

Souls, the *djinn* replied simply. *Three of them.*

Here now I beg your forgiveness as I pause in the midst of the young man's tale and at such an inopportune time. But I have told you so much of his journey and so little of the story's other participant that I worry you may have forgotten the king and his indefatigable army.

You may protest that I have told you plenty of him, of his army's brutal march across the continent. Man is so accustomed to war, why should this be any different?

It is terrible enough when one is greedy for that which is not his, dishonorable when he steals it away, evil when he takes it through violence. Yet those are events that have beginnings and endings, they occur one moment and are over the next. What the king and his army wrought was far worse. Not content to merely capture the lands that were not his, the king sought to crush them; like an unruly child stomping over ants, simply to hear the crunch of their demise.

ॐ

I have said before that the young man was clever and so he did not recoil in horror as was his first inclination. *He needed only one wish so he would give only one soul*, the young man countered. For he was more than willing to give up his own so that his beloved could live.

But the *djinn* shook its head. The young man had misunderstood. It would not offer three wishes for three souls. *Three souls were needed for one wish and one wish only would be given*, it explained.

Now the young man could not withhold his revulsion, for he was a kind man and bore no ill against anyone. What's more, he could picture the despair upon his beloved's face if ever she discovered the cost of her cure and that image caused him an even greater pain. Yet the thought of his beloved's continued suffering was an un-healing wound both in his heart and in his head.

He shook his head violently, though not even he could say if it were in denial of the *djinn's* offer or to clear the image of his love's anguish from his mind. Staggering under the sudden weight of despair he could not push aside, he stumbled back the way he had come, hurtling himself from the chilled shadows back into the sultry warmth.

ॐ

But night had fallen and the desert's stifling heat had been broken.

ॐ

It was not until he reached into his satchel for his tinderbox that the young man realized he still held the *djinn's* mystery object in his hand; a small dagger with a blade barely as long as the length of his hand and made of a glossy black metal that appeared as glass. *Souls,* he heard in the *djinn's* silky voice, *three of them.*

He shuddered and set the weapon aside, turning his attention to building a fire that would ward off the coldness that had burrowed inside of him. It was not long before he had crackling flames dancing near his feet, warming his face and bringing light to his small patch of darkness.

That was not all it brought.

ॐ

Whether it was the fire that drew him forth or some whimsy of that force men call fate my story will not say. But it was not long after the young man had crafted his moderate blaze that it caught the attention of a desert bandit, one of those devilish characters who carve out their existence by theft and violence.

The young man was just drowsing off when he felt the wiry arm wrap around his throat and squeeze. Instantly awake, he clawed at the limb crushing his airway and rolled forward, flipping the bandit over his shoulder. They both landed on their backs with echoing grunts, the impact forcing the assailant to release his grip.

But faster than the young man thought possible the bandit was astride him, hands closing around the young man's throat.

His lungs beginning to burn, the young man dug at the fingers gripping him with one hand while the other desperately searched the sands nearby for any aid that the desert was willing to share. A rock, a dwarf cactus, anything. Just as his vision began to go white at the edges his fingers closed over smooth leather. Blindly he punched up into the bandit's side and felt the ruffian stiffen immediately. The hands around his throat loosened and fell away.

ॐ

The blade of the dagger glowed with a light that did not come from the fire's embers. The young man stared at it and once again heard the *djinn's* lilting voice within his head. *Three souls for one wish.*

ॐ

Were Fate kinder, I could tell you that the young man gathered the

9

rest of the *djinn's* payment through similar circumstance. For men who live lives of hate and deceit are rarely mourned and to save the life of one such as the young man's beloved was a far greater use of their souls than their own twisted devices.

But Fate is not kind. She is not calm or polite or even remotely caring. No man, not even one as true as this one, escapes her tangled web.

The young man walked for many days in search of those villains whose mere existence taints the world and whose presence the world can do very well without. He searched with such focus and fervor that he failed to the feel the burn of the sun against his skin and the lightening of his waterskins until it was far too late.

For a moment it seemed a mirage, a trick of the desert played upon his weary eyes. It was rare enough to see a camel-borne palanquin; few in the desert owned enough to warrant one in their travels. But it was even rarer to see one upended, contents spilled across the sand and the beast of burden splayed out unmoving beside it.

As he drew closer, the young man saw the father first. He lay stretched out, almost atop the structure, as if protecting it. His arms were crossed in front of his face but neither they nor the heavy wrappings around his head had kept away Death.

Stepping forward, the young man pushed aside the curtains of the palanquin, revealing the mother and the little girl clasped in her arms. Again, Death had not been stayed. As he shifted to release the curtain, the eyes of the mother fluttered open and locked with his. Almost imperceptibly her lips moved but no words made it past the parched skin. The young man frantically dug into his satchel and despaired as each waterskin he removed proved to be empty.

Their eyes met again, his full of sorrow and hers filled with pain. She barely had the strength to keep her eyes open, but her arms tightened around the body of her child. And the pain in her gaze transformed into a desperate pleading that squeezed his heart.

Again the dagger's blade glowed. *Three souls for one wish.*

Serving as both a bitter reward and a mocking punishment the desert gave one of its rarest jewels that night.

It rained. Sheets of water that cascaded down from the sky. The young man stood out in the storm and methodically held open each of his waterskins, waiting patiently for the thick leather to grow heavy. The water poured over him, shockingly cold against the heat the desert sun had burned into his skin. He blinked it from his eyes and carefully set the stopper once each drinking pouch was full. With no sense of urgency he stowed them away in his satchel, positioning them thoughtfully, though there was little else in the bag to compete with for space.

When there was no more arranging to be done, he set the satchel aside and, sinking his head into his hands, he added his tears to the desert's rain.

࿇

Here, now, finally, our two stories intertwine. The young man soon found himself once more at the crossroads just outside the tiny village where he had met the old beggar man. Weeks had passed but the beggar remained the same; it was the scene behind him that had drastically changed. The village huts were now pillars of flame and the quiet shuffling villagers were now barking soldiers.

But the ancient beggar still sat cross-legged, the wooden bowl still set out before him, two gold coins still its only occupants. His head lifted as the young man approached and this time his eyes were open, revealing two milky white orbs.

Behind the beggar the smoke from the fires stained the sky grey; the entire western horizon was dark, as if the king's army had crushed out the sun. The young man could see the line of soldiers snake back into the darkness and could well imagine the destruction their unrelenting march had wrought.

3, 4, 1. 3, 4, 1, the beggar murmured, his blind gaze tracking some movement only he could see. *3, 4, 1.*

࿇

One last time the dagger's blade glowed. *Three for one.*

࿇

The young man's journey back to the *djinn's* cave took no longer than it had the first time, though the burden he carried upon his heart

11

was thrice as heavy. All around him the desert was filled with the king's army, its violent deeds scarring the landscape. He slipped between them unseen, cloaked by his own newly earned darkness or perhaps the twisted kindness of Fate.

But although they did not see him, the young man could not help but witness the horrors the soldiers carried out in their king's name. And so it was a long three days of burning villages and fleeing folk before he once again stood bathed in the *djinn's* eerie blue light. Wordlessly the young man held forth the strange dagger; the red sheen from the blade played upon his hands like the blood he had, three times, so fervently scrubbed from his skin.

The *djinn* held up one elegant hand and, tipping its head slightly, made a small sweeping gesture that said, *make your wish.*

☙◦❧

In the following instant, the young man thought of many things. He thought of his beloved, of the gentle tone of her voice, even when rasping through the illness. He thought of her smile, of the cascading joy of her laughter renewed, and the sweetness of her kiss. He saw her strong and healthy, once more dancing over the desert sand with the sun of their future at her back.

Even as the blissful images flittered through his mind, he thought of the king's army, of its unyielding advance. He thought of the blackened villages and the news of worse to come. He thought of destroyed homes and lives and conquered broken people. He thought of the lives lost and those left to lose. He saw the madman's march as it crawled across the land, inching towards his own tiny village.

Unbidden, the young man's mind conjured up the bandit, his death grimace gruesome in the flickering firelight. He saw again the dying mother's arms wrapped tightly around her child and the old beggar's body stretched out along the road.

He saw himself fleeing with his beloved, her arms around his waist and her legs moving swiftly beneath her. He saw the desert sand white and pristine, the sky a piercing blue.

☙◦❧

Looking into the flickering blue of the *djinn's* gaze, the young man made his wish.

12

Scythe's Fate

Nicole DeGennaro

tatistician, I need you.

S   Lorna sat up in her chair, where she had dozed off. Being a constantly on-call telepath meant she had to sneak in catnaps when she could, so her chair often served as her bed, and she often suffered from a stiff neck.

I'm here, she replied after taking a sip from her cup of cold coffee. *Patching in.*

For Lorna, it was that easy to cross thousands of miles, multiple continents and oceans, or, on rare occasions, light-years to connect with a fellow superhero and offer assistance. They didn't need her telepathy, though; they needed her other ability.

It never gets any less weird having you in my head, Rubber Band Man said to her as she peered out through his eyes at the situation.

Can't be helped. He faced a collapsing building and a ticking bomb, far enough apart that even a superhero who could stretch himself great distances would only have the time to stop one catastrophe. Lorna would have to tell him which one to prevent.

Did Quandary set this up? she asked as she appraised the situation. *If so, he hasn't claimed credit yet.*

Statistician? Another hero reached out to her.

On a call. You're up next, she shot back. After evaluating Rubber Band Man's conundrum, her second power had kicked in. It only took a few seconds, and then the numbers appeared over each situation; when a predicament involved groups of people instead of single potential victims, the provided number gave an average of their worth. The universe put the

15

two (or three or twelve) choices on a set of invisible scales and showed Lorna which would have the better outcome in the long run.

At least, that was what she had come to believe. After five decades with the ability—it always took her by surprise to realize she was nearly seventy-five—she still could only guess at how it worked. By now, she knew to trust the numbers. The universe kept its inputs to itself, showing her only its solutions.

The bomb, she said.

But there are more people—

The bomb, Rubber Band Man. You asked me, and I'm telling you. As he sprang into action, she signed off with her standard, *Until next time.*

She pulled out of his mind, trusting him to handle the rest. He could make whatever choice he wanted if he had doubts—although she found that the younger heroes rarely defied her decisions. They didn't want to be responsible for the repercussions.

When she returned to her own head, she gasped, then blinked in the harsh fluorescent light. After those few moments of adjusting, she departed once more.

You're up, she said, reaching out to the superhero who had summoned her earlier. She rode the thread of that call like a zip line; when she brushed against the other mind, she recognized it as Supersonica. *I hope this isn't a social call.*

No, Supersonica said. *I need what only you can do.* Lorna looked through her eyes at a burning school. This would be more difficult, but in the end the universe would calculate an answer.

Other superheroes en route, Supersonica said. *Just not sure when they'll arrive.*

The fire had already compromised the structure of the school. Although Supersonica would be able to save more than one of the kids and teachers trapped inside, she wouldn't be able to save them all.

I need you in the air, Lorna said. She could make Supersonica's body do it herself, but she aimed to work with the superheroes who requested her help, not make them feel possessed. Supersonica did as she asked, and from above Lorna could see the whole school. Although she couldn't see the individual people inside, the universe knew. It always did.

After perhaps a whole minute, although it felt much longer as the fire raged, the numbers appeared. She directed Supersonica from the highest to the lowest as best she could. By the time backup arrived, only a few minutes later, the building had collapsed. Supersonica and Lorna had saved twenty-one of the one-hundred and three people stuck inside.

She disconnected from Supersonica without her sign-off and sat back in her chair with her eyes closed. Fire engulfed the darkness of her mind.

҈

Lorna's generation had been the first to manifest superpowers, and when she had been growing up it seemed that every other teenager could suddenly fly or teleport or manipulate plants. A few decades after the so-called Superpower Boom, enough studies had been done for there to be an official estimate: about one percent of her generation worldwide had ended up with superpowers. However, researchers further estimated that no more than half of the one percent had lived long enough for said powers to activate. Still, considering the world population, the boom had resulted in a plethora of superheroes—and supervillains. Since then, the percentage had decreased each generation until plateauing at so low a rate that new superpowered people had become uncommon.

She had been a late bloomer; during a time when everyone thought the manifestation of superpowers coincided with puberty, Lorna hadn't become a telepath until twenty-five, and she hadn't known right away that she had two powers. The telepathy was secondary, meant to facilitate her ability to see the worth the universe assigned to everyone.

At first she hadn't realized what the numbers meant. Then, when they only appeared in life-or-death situations, she began to suspect their significance. Even with the hunch, it took years for her to accept that, without fail, the numbers were right. It had been a long and perhaps foolish experiment on her part, born partly from disbelief and partly from denial and a desire to avoid the inherent responsibility that accompanied the power. In the beginning of her superhero career, she had sometimes chosen the lower number when her emotions contradicted the universe's calculations. And by now she had outlived most of those saved victims, in some cases by decades; others had gone on to become supervillains, terrorists, murderers. So after a few years of testing the numbers and failing, she had accepted the universe's infallibility.

Her defiant streaks had at least revealed that lifespan and likelihood of becoming a threat to others influenced the universe's calculation of someone's worth. Even with that knowledge, Lorna still struggled with the idea that when it came down to it, everyone could be assigned a number—the universe did not see all humans as equal.

Five decades at it had made her constantly weary; she longed to retire, to pass the mantle of The Statistician to a younger superhero with the same powers. Most of her contemporaries who had survived had retired when a new, younger superhero with the same or similar powers came along. But Lorna had not yet met her successor. Perhaps she would not be replaced. Once she died, maybe the new superheroes would have to make their own impossible decisions.

On her more exhausting days, in her more bitter moods, she thought about closing up shop regardless. Didn't she deserve a few happy years after all the work she had put in? She never could follow through, though, even with other superheroes—and supervillains—making that choice. Her conscience wouldn't let her. It would be criminal to have a power like hers and not use it.

However, she had never foreseen having to use her power as often as she had in the last decade. Her contemporaries had always used her sparingly, only in the most dire situations. But as they passed their knowledge of her onto the newer heroes, Lorna found herself called upon more and more often, sometimes even when the proper course of action would be clear to anyone. Her days had become filled with a never-ending wait list of superheroes needing help.

She couldn't hold on to her frustration at her overuse, though. The memories of the euphoria of the Superpower Boom shone clear as glass in her mind—and her recollection of the subsequent crash ran through them like a crack: the rash of superhero suicides when they couldn't live with the decisions they had been forced to make; abilities so powerful and uncontrollable that they drove the person insane or killed them; the surge in supervillains when the powered decided it was easier to cause rather than prevent chaos.

It hadn't taken long for the powered to realize the sad truth behind their gifts: no matter how many superheroes existed, they could not save everyone.

If the universe did have some way to maintain its fragile homeostasis, perhaps the manifestation of her powers had been a course correction. A way to keep the superpowered population from wiping itself out. It had been tricky for her at first—the superheroes who had managed to survive the worst of the crash had created their own decision-making methods and coping mechanisms that her existence negated. Some had accused her of being a villain until she had proven herself, and then they had realized she could take the responsibility off them. Reliably. Consistently. After that, the superheroes had not wanted to remember they had ever operated without her.

So the existence of The Statistician had become a piece of knowledge the old heroes passed on to their protégés. However, like Lorna, they had no real idea how her power worked. They knew even less about it than she did. She didn't crunch numbers or have some algorithm to calculate someone's worth. But few heroes ever asked her to explain her abilities, and by the time various world governments had each organized a branch to handle the superpowered, Lorna and her generation had been grandfathered in. When someone did ask her for details, she stuck with the mythos that everyone else had established: complicated math, nothing more.

She didn't want to get into lengthy half-explanations, and she worried that if the truth of her powers got out, it would cause a different type of crisis—a spiritual one. Lorna had never been religious, and she didn't believe her ability indicated the existence of a higher power. Everything in the universe, at every level, had a way of maintaining its own homeostasis that operated passively or subconsciously, and she didn't see why the universe as a whole should function differently than even its tiniest part. But it would be easy, too easy, to see her ability as proof of either the existence or the nonexistence of a higher power, and she wanted no part of that conversation.

Her abilities had already complicated her life enough, given her enough burdens. At first she had tried, like most of those in the boom, to lead a double life; they had used the old comic book superheroes as a template. By the time she had hit thirty, however, the dichotomy had become intolerable. Knowing everyone could be reduced down to a number made it hard for her to interact with anyone.

Being a telepath didn't help, either. People's emotions seeped out of their minds like sweat from the skin; it couldn't be controlled. Despite the mental barriers Lorna had built to protect herself, she could sense the leaks all the same. With the Superpower Boom and crash, most people on the planet were related to superheroes or supervillains, or had lost someone to a battle between the two. And, more often than not, Lorna had been involved in that battle, had made the call on who to save.

So she had withdrawn from her attempt at a normal life until nobody called, nobody came to her door. Then she moved to her current gated, out-of-the-way home, where she only interacted with the grocery delivery man once a week for a few minutes. Technology and telepathy replaced other interactions: e-mail instead of snail mail, direct deposit of her checks from the superhero union, telepathy to do her job. On the occasions Lorna needed a doctor, she came to her, although Lorna put those visits off as long as possible. Isolating herself protected her from sensing nebulous emotions related to lost loved ones that she knew should be directed at her. It also kept her from stumbling across any sudden situations—car accidents, house fires and the like—that might reveal people's numbers.

She no longer remembered who had coined the misnomer The Statistician for her; some hero or other had called her that and it had stuck. But it had never felt right to Lorna. She had always called herself The Scythe.

⇦⇨

Statistician?

This time Lorna had made it to her bed for a quick nap before being roused by the call. The superhero didn't have to be a telepath to reach her; they just had to send a message into the ether. Lorna had realized shortly after her telepathy had activated that superpowered brainwaves operated on a slightly different frequency than those of normal people. She had a blacklist of known villains and wove those into her barriers to protect herself from attack. Thus, she could leave her mind open to heroes while filtering out most other psychic noise.

I'm here, she said as she made her way to her chair; she supposed she could work from her bed, really, but the chair had been specially designed to keep her body in place and comfortable when she had to send her mind off to someone else's body.

Once in her chair, she followed the psychic trail to the superhero who had reached out to her. Supersonica again, although she seemed to be off duty.

A social call? Lorna asked.

If you have the time.

Lorna smiled; many superheroes ended up isolated like her, and her nearly universal presence made her an appealing person to talk with. She didn't mind.

I do. What's going on? She could have dug around; some of it already stood out to her—doubts and frustrations seeped from the dark corners of Supersonica's mind. Lorna always did her best to respect boundaries, though. She didn't snoop around in the subconscious.

You disconnected kind of abruptly before. Are you all right?

She got up to make herself some coffee. Because it was a social call, she didn't have to do anything more than connect to Supersonica's mind—as simple as picking up a phone, for a telepath.

It never gets easier knowing you can't save them all, Lorna said. When she had been younger, she had wanted to seem invincible, as if the guilt didn't affect her. She had adopted the "coolly disconnected from humanity" façade. After isolating herself, she had no longer seen the point in pretending. Even with her guidance, many of the superheroes she helped still struggled with the choices they made. That guilt and the powers themselves served as the last two connections she had with any part of humanity at large, and she didn't want to deny them.

Every time I put on my costume, I think this will be the time I finally do manage to save everyone, Supersonica said, her bitterness ringing clear in Lorna's head.

People always considered psychic communication to be devoid of feeling because it lacked inflection, but Lorna found it more expressive. Emotions clung to the words as they crossed from one mind to the other. There could be no misinterpretation, no deception. When the words landed in her mind, their impact craters dispersed the attached emotion into her psyche. She didn't have to guess if Supersonica felt frustration or resentment. She knew it as clearly as if they were her own emotions.

It'll be much easier if you accept your limits. It's just not possible. Even with the superpower disillusionment experienced by Lorna's generation, the public relations machine of superpowerdom still pushed the ideal of the just, flawless superhero who could save everyone. People wanted their heroes to be uncomplicated beacons of hope. But complication defined the human condition, and she had not yet met someone with the power to negate that fact.

Supersonica didn't reply; still, Lorna didn't have to wonder if the connection had been cut. Despite the silence, she could feel Supersonica's emotional leakage.

I might be the only person who always wishes for a world-threatening meteor or something, Lorna continued, hoping to shift the conversation away, just slightly, from the fallacy of the infallible hero.

You're not the only one, Supersonica said. *That's when being a superhero is simple. Those are the times we just do what we do: save the world.*

This isn't meant to be easy, Supersonica, Lorna said. She knew all the superheroes' real names, whether she wanted to or not. However, she avoided using them. Even if a superhero said she could; even if she sometimes got sentimental about some of the younger ones. She did it to keep her distance—the same reason she never wanted to know personal information about anyone—because someday she might have to decide if one of those heroes lived or died. After all, sometimes the supervillains got the upper hand. *The heroic part is sticking with it. The alternative would be to know you could make a difference in the world and to choose not to.*

Sometimes that seems better.

It wouldn't be. If it hadn't been for you, all of those children and teachers in the school fire would have died. You couldn't save them all, but twenty-one survived thanks to you.

Her coffee had finished percolating, so she poured herself a cup while she waited out the silence from Supersonica.

How have you dealt with this for so long? I mean, you're the one who makes the choice for all of us.

Supersonica was not the first superhero to ask that question of her, although it was one of the few times she considered trying to formulate an honest yet not too depressing answer. She had had decades to learn to cope, but as she aged and waited for her successor—and vacillated between hoping there would be one and hoping there wouldn't—she wondered if the methods she had chosen to deal with her powers had been best. They had kept her alive, at least, which couldn't be said for many of her contemporaries.

Well, it's more complicat—

Statistician! Another superhero called for her before she could finish, or rather start, her explanation.

Sorry, Supersonica, she said, not just as a formality. She had been looking forward to having a frank discussion about her coping mechanisms with someone. *I'm being called away.*

Convenient, Supersonica said. The playfulness came through clear. *Go save some people, Statistician. And thanks for the chat.*

I hope it helped. Until next time.

�⚬⚬�

The next time came quickly; it always did. If a supervillain wasn't causing havoc, then superheroes turned their attention to preventing the everyday hostilities between the nonpowered. Even those came with choices: stop the sexual assault or the hostage situation or the mugging or the murder? By now, the superheroes knew Lorna could only help with life-threatening situations. If someone was going to survive a mugging or assault, the universe told her nothing about that person's worth. Unfortunately, Lorna had long ago learned that she could always find some fatal decision to be made somewhere.

Statistician, are you there? She had been putting her delivered groceries away when the call came. She always started with the refrigerator and freezer items, and luckily she had already finished with them. She left the rest in their bags as she went to her chair. Then she followed the open line until she connected once more with Supersonica.

She appeared to be in a confrontation with the supervillain Quandary. If each superhero had a nemesis, Lorna suspected Quandary was meant to be hers, although she doubted he knew she existed. He spent his time setting up impossible choices for the superheroes, always giving them a chance to save one set of victims or no victims but never all of them. Somehow he always knew how many and which heroes would respond— and thus what powers he would have to counteract with his traps.

I hate this guy, Lorna said.

Tell me about it. Supersonica hovered high enough to allow Lorna to survey the situation. A young man and woman each dangled precariously over separate deadly traps. An elaborate pulley system connected the two people; they served as each other's counterbalance. If Supersonica cut one loose, the other would succumb to their trap. With her power set, there would be no way to pull the bindings through the pulleys with a person still attached, and the people had been spaced too far apart for her to save both.

Still Lorna felt vague and unwanted relief that there would only be one casualty; Quandary tended to aim for a high death toll. She just hoped there wouldn't be a surprise.

No other heroes nearby to help, I presume, she said.

Only me and you.

All right then.

Lorna focused on the two captives, but then she noticed the catch: the man and woman were brother and sister; she could easily see the family resemblance in the shape of their mahogany eyes, the slope of their noses, their matching desperate expressions. They could not have been older than twenty. So Quandary would get two victims no matter what—at best, one living and one dead.

She kept that to herself in case Supersonica did not already know and went back to concentrating. The young woman made eye contact with Supersonica and thus with Lorna. Instead of crying or screaming or cursing, the woman's expression shifted to one of quiet resignation.

A moment later, the universe revealed the numbers to Lorna: it valued the brother more by a wide margin. She sighed.

Before she could deliver the information to Supersonica, though, another presence brushed against her mind. Lorna paused, wary. The contact had been too timid to be another superhero seeking help yet too sloppy and passive to be an attack from Quandary or an accomplice. She hoped.

Hello? the unknown person said.

Lorna hesitated to answer. The message had a clear, solid sound in her head, indicating it had been sent directly to her, a skill that only another telepath would have. When the other superheroes called out to her, they broadcast their messages without focus, like using a global megaphone. Any listening telepath could hear their calls. When Lorna connected to their minds, she secured the line, so to speak, with barriers and methods of masking that she had learned and honed over time. This telepath had opened a new, private line with Lorna without alerting Supersonica.

She didn't recognize the brainwaves, meaning she had never interacted with this telepath before. Without thinking, she turned Supersonica's gaze to Quandary for a moment, but he had become too absorbed in some rant or taunt to be the one contacting her. The other telepath had to be someone nearby, though; Lorna could tell from the strength and clarity of the attempted connection.

You all right? Supersonica asked, and Lorna realized her faux pas.

Sorry. I got distracted. Give me another minute. Keep Quandary occupied. I just need the two kids in your line of vision.

Sure, no problem.

The young man struggled against his bindings, yelling and crying. The young woman, however, remained calm and kept her eyes on Supersonica.

Hello? I don't know if this is working, the same person said. Lorna shored up her defenses and followed the connection until she reached the young woman's mind.

Yes; I'm here, she replied, making sure to stay vigilant, keeping all her barriers up and blocking access to Supersonica's mind as protection.

The numbers still lingered by the woman and her brother. The difficulty of Lorna's job had just increased exponentially knowing that the woman, whom Lorna had been moments away from allowing to die, also had powers. Yet her brother, who seemed normal, still had more worth to the universe.

I heard Supersonica call out to you, so I knew you were there in her head. I just...I just wanted to let you know it's okay, the woman said.

Statistician? Why is this taking so long? Supersonica asked.

What's okay? Lorna asked the young woman. Then, *I'm sorry; there's a complication,* to Supersonica.

Is there something you need me to do to help? Supersonica asked. Lorna answered in the negative, but she knew she was running out of time to listen to what this woman had to say.

What you have to do, the young woman said. *I understand. I can see the numbers too.*

Oh hell, Lorna said before she could stop herself, accidentally broadcasting it to Supersonica and the young woman—the person who could have been Lorna's protégé; the only other person she had ever met with her same powers.

What? What is it? Supersonica asked. Lorna couldn't come up with anything to say to her or the young woman. The numbers remained the same, leaving no question about the right action. And Lorna knew too well what happened when she went against the universe.

What's your name? Lorna asked the young woman.

Alma. Alma Palomo.

Statistician! Quandary knows I'm stalling. I need a choice, please. Now.

Lorna looked at Alma in Supersonica's peripheral vision. To let her die would be to leave the superheroes without a Scythe, a Statistician, when Lorna died. She didn't know if that would be a bad thing; it seemed to be what the universe wanted. Maybe the time had come for the heroes to once more shoulder the responsibility of making their own decisions.

But Alma saw the numbers. She understood. Lorna could train her; for a time they could share the burden. Then Lorna could fade into the background, retire from service. Alma could decide to wean the superheroes off their dependency on The Statistician or maintain the status quo. Lorna couldn't ignore the part of her that wanted to save Alma despite the numbers, that wanted to defy the universe's detestable system of balance one last time.

I'm sorry, Lorna said, to everyone. Then she cut her connection with Alma. After taking a second to collect herself, she told Supersonica who to save.

Until next time, she said to Supersonica as she signed off, knowing there wouldn't be one, knowing she had made her final choice.

Shared Wall

Christopher Rogers

We can build whatever we want to make this our home. We can build our own home." I remember then-wide-eyed Brandon saying. He and PH Stephen lived in the first room so we could have a little privacy as ladies, which I thought was nice.

Four art school graduates in what was technically a two-bedroom apartment was a luxury. These days, I'm hearing six and eight. We had all just left the dorms, but why change a thing? I love paying too much for shitty living conditions.

Amy and I decided that we should build something of a shared wall because we kept such different hours: I, the late sleeper, the midnight toker, would take the far back room, which meant I got the window, but meant I'd have to tip-toe in if anyone actually had to wake up for work the next day, which I think happened twice.

Amy and I built the shared wall from sheets of drywall and acoustic tiles that we covered with a sort of scratchy orange corduroy. When we were done, I felt like we'd only just begun collaborating.

I was ecstatic. Amy shut the door.

The boys ended up not caring about division, so I only ended up having to carefully navigate two rooms with eyes averted, "respectfully" open and close three doors, and wash a lot of dishes.

I started working under Ferdinand Meyer pretty quickly—maybe you've heard of him—and how he manipulates metal is insane. Anyway, he liked the cages I made as my thesis project: "They're Celtic myths in spun glass." Except they were aluminum, but I knew what he meant.

Maybe I should've planned ahead and graduated in January.

Working with him meant long days—even though they started at noon—in a hotbox garage in the ass-end-of-nowhere part of Astoria. The summer was breaking century-old records almost every day, but we were onto something.

"I almost always discover why I can't work with an assistant for long."

I giggled, which is really stupid, but I did. OK?

"But I'm trusting your work and this week has been great, but we're telling—" Basically, he warned me that he's demanding and he usually works with girls and I got the sense that he does more with girls than make "poetry in metal, which so few can do."

And I didn't want to stop, so I kept an eye out for his wandering hands, but tried not to burn my fingers off at the same time.

I started going in early, still working twelve-plus-hour days. While moving around some of the pipes and sheets we're using has made my arms look great, I lost a lot of weight because I drank for dinner; the four of us all tried to keep in regular touch. All summer, we drank on our roof—another reason why we took the place—and would catch up, commiserate, and make fun of each other.

"Wanna make poetry with me, Lila?" Amy let drip out of her mouth. The boys about died. Whatever, I kissed her. She recoiled though and pretended to vomit. I didn't think it was that bad. What? We went to college to learn.

Anyway. A couple of beers later, Amy let out more than fake barf:

"Dude, if I don't find a job, I'm gonna fucking die, because that's all I can do before I ask my dad for money and become a fucking stereotype."

"What are you more worried about," PH Stephen managed, "what other people think about you, or having to forfeit your first step into adulthood, by which I mean—"

"Psychology double-major over here is inviting you, when you're ready and want to make the choice, to reach the conclusion that everything and everyone can fuck off," Amy continued, but they were always finishing each other's sentences. "You'll figure it out and make it work in the meantime."

She swigged. Hell, we all swigged.

"I can cover you through September, no problem." I said. We all paid $600 each.

"Fuck that, we all can," one of the boys said.

She made a lot of calls that night. At first, I was too polite and I let the acoustic tiles do their duty, but as she called into the night with hushed tones and my lights were off, the seams around the edges shone with her burning midnight oil. I cozied up to one of them and put my ear just about against it and, "It's all about who you know, I guess? Reggie, don't fuck with me. Don't fucking do this to—OK. Yeah, no. You're right. I just—that's a lot of fucking money. Where? Where Irving becomes Moffat? That's total sketchville. And by that cemetery—How long would I have to be there? Five minutes? I blocked the number because I share this phone, so you can't just call it whenever, OK? It's 341—" and I pull away because I already know the phone number. She shares the phone with me.

∿✿∿

I'm a child again that night when I have a dream about my dad. He was welding huge wings for a plane—kinda true to life—and as I move closer and closer to him, I'm high on the same ideas of freedom I'd have when I thought about the wings we could make for me. Sparks and a dimly lit hangar wrinkle his entire being with harsh shadows.

The rivets are flush and the run my fingers along the nearly invisible seams. I don't know how or why he's doing this alone, but it's excellent work.

He notices me and dials down the flame. As I stare back at the solid black line of his mask, he moves closer to me, almost gliding across from the other end of the wing. He uses the back of his free hand to lift his mask. He is a shadow of himself, literally. He wraps his one arm around me, torch still alight in his dominant hand.

"Make poetry with me, Lila," his eyes bearing their own flame, his skin an even duller grey, the surrounding shadows slowly pulling him apart. "We can make them see. We can make new language, a new world. We can do the impossible."

I wake breathless because I remember how real it is that he's gone.

I end up with the phone somehow.

I forgot to take it out of my pocket and it's vibrating so loudly on the floor. I see on my alarm clock that it's 3:23 and retch out a groggy hello into the hastily grabbed box of light and noise.

"Yeah, Amy girl. You gotta get down here."

"Down where?"

"We talked about this. If you want the $600, you gotta get yourself down here right now. You know where the presents is at. Marcus is gonna meet—" but I pull the phone away from my ear because Amy is knocking on the shared wall's door, though casually.

I open it, peeking only my head around.

"Do you have the phone? I'm expecting a call."

"Yeah, here—I answered it by accident. I was asleep." I hand it to her, but as it passes by my ear, I hear an agitated voice.

"Cool, thanks," and she pulls the door shut.

I lean up against the shared wall and she says a few things, firstly apologizing for it not being she who answered, that she's ready to go, that she'll deliver it as promised.

How much are they making that they can give her $600 for it in one run? Why am I welding all summer if --

But I fall asleep.

It feels like a wink when the alarm goes off again, 10:15 as usual. The apartment is always empty at this time so who cares about covering up, clothes at all, before leaving? Who cares about make-up, even, as I'll just sweat it off? Doubling up on deodorant, though.

I'm out by 10:45. I get an Americano on the corner. It's waiting for me before I get there. I smile, say thank you, tip as usual and go. I'm halfway through my commute before I realize I don't even have my keys. We just pull the door shut because we don't really have anything to steal. Someone will probably be home later, but I can already feel my heart wrenching.

I get to work and nothing is set up. The whole floor is basically empty. It's the first time I notice the floor, actually, as it's been covered with all of our shit to do.

What remains is all covered in those bold blue tarps from any construction project. They're draped in heaps over several mounds of whatever. I approach one slowly, like it's alive and waiting to rip me apart. I lift up the shorter parts of it and I see the familiar colors and bends I was afraid of seeing; there are tarps all over our "poetry," our time together brutally dismantled.

"Ferdinand."

"You make so much goddamn noise," I hear over my shoulder. I smell him before I see him, alcohol radiating from his skin. I turn on my boot heels and bear down on him.

"What the hell happened?"

"It's not us."

"What's not us?"

"It was too derivative, too referential, too vague at the same time," and he went on mumbling, looking beyond the tarp stacks.

"What are we going to work on today, then?" I'm a little too angry.

"Go home."

But I just stand there.

He puts his left arm around me, that hand on my back. He holds his other shaking palm open, not as if to smack me, but as if the fire he once held burned him. "I said go home." And he pulls me closer.

I think about all of the posters at school—

Learn to S-I-N-G: Solar plexus, Instep, Nose, Groin—

And I almost do, but he lets me go.

We stare into each other's eyes for a while and that's when I see that he doesn't want to fuck me. I see that we share the same loss, we mourn the same work, and we know we can never make the same thing again. Even though he destroyed it, he feels it a hundred times more.

I'd drink, too. It's all I want to do.

I take his advice. I go home. I walk there, take the long way. By the time I get home, PH Stephen is there, buzzes me in, leaves the door open. He's in his tiny boxer briefs in the one chair at our tiny kitchen table. "They're in the bathroom," he says kind of chuckling. "Thank you," I say and I go in, get two beers, and raise them above my head triumphantly as I make my way back through the rooms. I have a thought as I open the door on the shared wall.

"You know where the presents is at."

Is it on the phone? I never read the text messages because everyone just e-mails me or calls. PH Stephen starts a shower almost on cue and I steel myself to dig through Amy's shit and it's not long before I find a diary and a couple of sex toys, but not even a joint surfaces in places I'd keep my most private things.

"The presents." The presence? Something not seen but felt...

The shared wall isn't very thick, but I notice the head of her bed meets the shared wall in a funny way. It kind of leans out on an extended shadow and one of the felt tiles is sticking out. I try not to move the bed, but I also don't want to move the tile. I reach back there, blindly, like all horror films have taught me not to do, and that's when I feel the presence. I pull it out and immediately panic because I'm using my bare hands to handle a pure white, plastic-wrapped brick of something out of a crime drama.

The longer I stare at it, the heavier it seems to be, the closer I bring it to my face. It's wrapped like a Christmas gift and maybe in some weird way it belongs to me, since there isn't a tag with a name. I notice the seams where sheer tape is raggedly cut. It looks easy enough to peel back, put back on, but again it's all about fingertips—just don't touch the sticky side—and before I know it, the flap is open. I stick my nose inside like an idea and the sweet smell tricks my body into taking a deep sniff.

And I already want more.

I'm back in my room with the door shut and locked, the window covered. I've somehow ended up with the Presence in my arms like a baby and I'm thinking about how to hold on to the initial rush without going over the edge. I'm thinking about how close I can play, how much I can rub up against the edge before it breaks the skin, leaves a scar.

But fuck it. I don't know what's going on anymore.

I'll just do like a pea-sized amount, like toddlers and toothpaste.

I hold out the open flap as much as I can without spilling any and push a very, very small amount of the powder forward and then it's

one-two-

three

and

I see stars. You can't see stars here and it's maybe the only other thing I miss about being back home. Constellations—their legends, their majestic failures—hanging in the sky, just waiting to be read, interpreted, misinterpreted. The room is dark, but I know it well enough to put the Presence down. I lean against the wall and I feel the entirety of my body buzzing. I feel the wall buzzing back, the sheets under me as I am cross-legged on my bed buzzing. My entire body waxes and wanes and trembles and it's like the first time I made love. It hasn't been love that I've made in a long time. My heart is aching as it reaches out to something I know is just beyond the shared wall and I want to bawl my eyes out, but that's when I feel it starting to fade.

Or maybe I'm getting used to it? Am I supposed to hold onto it?

I look over at the Presence. No, I shouldn't.

And I start laughing sort of without myself. That is, a bit of laughter comes out of me and I know it's right, but I didn't do it.

My arm reaches for it and I'm still like, "... no? Didn't you hear me? It's not right." But it's opening the flap again, drawing it down this time as it holds the brick just above my nose. Am I even supposed to snort this shit?

An avalanche of it is coming toward my face, but luckily time has slowed down. I'm able to take in maybe twice as much? Three times as much? I just manage to put it down before it hits again and holy fuck.

That's what a holy fuck feels like.

But there's something else. The heartache is back, but now I know what's pressing on it and it's actually in the shared wall. I lean up against it and listen. There's a scratching sound just as I press my ear to it that stops as I listen closer. I run my hands all over it and it comes back briefly—is it avoiding me?

"Hello?" I hear in a distant whisper from my own mouth.

Nothing. But as I smell the dust that's already started to accumulate on the acoustic tiles, I'm back in my backyard growing up. It's Memorial Day and Dad is grill master. Mom is calling from the window that "the veggies are done. Do you want a beer, honey?" and I'm torn between where I want to spend my time. I think I'm twelve years old. I must be, if Mom's there. I'm clinging to Dad's leg before I know it, which is stupid. He tells me to go inside and see if she needs help and I know he's right so I start to head inside. When I open the door—maybe it's my eyes adjusting or whatever—the inside is pitch black. I'm rubbing my eyes raw trying to see again and that's when I see the light of the torch again. I take only a few steps at first, but then I'm running towards it. It takes a long time to get even near it, so it's no surprise when it goes out. I slow to a stop, my aching, floppy feet clapping loudly on ... nothing?

Then two dots, the same hue, same size, are in front of me. I know immediately it's him, no longer healthy, no longer warm and filled with his own soul, his raison d'etre, his holy fuck, his magic, his love made.

"You know what you have to do," he says, as he approaches.

"No, I really don't."

"Make poetry, Lila," and by this point he's eleven feet tall, tall only to look down at me. "It's what you're good at."

"But I'm not. Ferdinand --"

"I didn't ask about Ferdinand. I didn't tell you to make poetry with him."

"But I'm not—"

"Lila, you really shouldn't be here," and he's looking over his shoulder because what we both need to be is paranoid right now. "I have to go."

And he just turns and starts walking away. "I have so much I need to tell you about! I have so many things I want to ask you!"

"But you aren't you, Lila. Are you?"

And it kind of pisses me off, but "How can I get back to you? How can I be myself?"

"You've already opened another door, haven't you?" He points to something but my eyes aren't working again. Everything is black. "Open up."

PH Stephen is knocking on the door, timidly, but insistently. "Are you OK?"

My eyes open and everything has little wisps and halos sitting on it.

"I'm fine, Stephen. I just need some time."

"Are you sure? We can talk."

"I don't want to talk." And I don't, but at least I didn't say everything's fine.

I hear his feet saunter far enough away that I'm finally able to take a deep, shaky breath.

Already opened another door.

Holy fuck, the drugs.

I fucking used something I stole from Amy.

I can't just put it back. What if I never put it back?

Won't she be in huge trouble without it?

Won't she be in huge trouble because I fucking used it?

What if I just come flat-out clean, tell her I went through her things, ask her about buying it? But I heard how much it costs.

What if I sell it and use that money to buy another brick, replace it before she finds out? Who do I know with that kind of money? Who could buy it within the next twelve hours?

No. I have to do better.

I stare at it, the flap open, soaking up the humid Brooklyn summer, and I remember.

The shared phone.

⊰⊱

"It's not a perfect kilo."

"The world isn't perfect. We had to make sure the product was."

"Oh, so you admit it? The King doesn't appreciate this kind of shit. Just saying."

"The King isn't here, is he? He sent you and I'm guessing you two can work it out."

"How about you give me some trim and I'll go home, level it off, and forget that you tried this shit with me?"

"I think you can go home and level it off without me. Use both hands if you have to."

"You know the price. You know what we what expected. There's less than that, so there should be a lower price. It's basic. If not a lower price, it's gotta be worth our while."

"Maybe this wasn't a good idea," I say and I nearly throw up.

"Why do you think they have skinny little bitches running this shit instead of cutting out the middle man? Part of the bargain."

"How about I just go home with my imperfect kilo? We were doing just fine."

"The King likes fire, little girl. And I've been in that rat trap where you sleep."

Right, so this isn't going well.

"All right, let's just ... what's your name?"

"Dudley."

"Dudley. All right. I think I started this off wrong with you and I'm sorry about that."

"Uh, yeah, you're not buying a purse in Chinatown, girl."

"And neither are you, so I thought we could chat about a bit about the price, but I didn't expect things to get so heated."

Maybe my jaw trembled or he saw my eye twitch or something because suddenly he says, "You haven't really negotiated before, have you? Just seen a lot of TV?"

I nod my head, which I know is stupid because if he is asking me to show my hand, he can see I have nothing.

"If I give you the keys, will you get in the car with me? I just want to talk and we're wasting a lot of time out here." I nod again; he puts a mass of brass and rings in my hand. I sit in the passenger seat, he's in the

37

driver's, but he's reaching into the back.

"Hunger in the body and hunger in the mind work the same way; we try to fill the nutritional, mental, or emotional voids in us hopefully as needed, but there are times when something, anything seems like the right answer."

He shuts something between the back seats. It's a pretty classy sedan with lots of compartments, so I'm guessing it's easy to lose track; in a pouch in the back of my seat, he reaches deep, moves some things around.

"I'm guessing the incomplete kilo has to do with that, right?"

He re-joins me, a sizeable blunt in hand.

"Now, I ain't mad. I just want to know what happened. In times of mental or emotional malnutrition, how far would we go when we're tempted by something that looks like an answer?"

He takes out a lighter wrapped in a brown cord, the long, free end bent over the opening for a flame.

"It's a hippie trick. You light the hemp cord so you don't get any butane in your smoke. I rolled this with hemp paper so you won't cough, because I'm guessing you've either never really smoked or you don't smoke on the regular."

And I just nod. Jesus.

"I also sprinkled in a little Presence, because I think that's the root of all of this, isn't it?"

He lights the damned thing and hits it hard, passes it to me.

"Come on down the rabbit hole," he chokes out of his voice box while holding as much smoke as he can in his lungs, "tell me what's on your mind." So, I take it. I stare at the red-hot ash on the end of what I'm guessing is very expensive. Out of obligation—and, OK, curiosity—I try to match his drag. It takes a minute, which is really fast, actually, because I have smoked before and know what pot does to me.

The Presence manifests as a warm fuzziness and—instead of coughing—I'm suddenly speaking somehow separate from myself, even while I'm screaming inside to shut the fuck up. I tell him almost everything: Ferdinand, never having friends growing up, my lesbian experience in high school, about how watching my blue-collar dad work made me want to create, about how losing him nearly killed me—all the while, we pass the smoke between us and I sink further.

It feels like six seconds pass; it feels like six hours pass.

The world starts to fade out as the dull, warm grey of my eyelids obscures everything outside. Inside, the smoke overtakes everything and I feel like I'm so busy catching up to what he's saying in response to what I've been spouting. He probably thinks I'm crazy.

I try to push through the smoke with all I have left, but I don't get anywhere.

My eyes start to focus on something just beyond the edge of how far I can see and I am reminded of introductory scenes in synchronized swimming TV specials. I can only see arms and legs doing something lost on me, but I try my best to get close to it. The smoke starts to settle onto things and take on their forms, everything still ghastly, but representing something super-familiar.

Sensations rush into me and give the beings and objects of smoke complete context: full-belly laughter reserved for childhood, skinned knees, discovery, elation, arousal, tears. Tears fall down my face as I realize it's my dad and me, but what we're doing keeps changing; one second he's tossing me into the air, catching me, but then he's Taking His Daughter to Work Day, teaching me how welding works. Mom even makes an appearance, so we're really spanning the years, but something lingers in the back of my mind consistently.

A blanketed, horizontal form.

I know it but don't want to know it. I know what it means.

I know that if I lift the sheet, it's over.

But I'm supposed to be all grown. I turn and face it and I try to stand up straight and show it I'm not afraid, but let's not be fucking stupid.

I draw nearer to it and it's very obviously a person underneath. It can't be anything else. It's not breathing. It doesn't shift at all, even as I stand right over it. I reach a tentative hand over it.

And slowly
slowly
slowly
slower than time
slower than slowly
put my hand on where the hand should be
and there is a hand
but it doesn't function

at all like a hand
it doesn't put mine
in its
it doesn't anything.

And it's cold as anything long dead, I guess, cold as his hands all-too-neatly folded on his chest, a rosary holding them together. Did you know they break a dead person's fingers so they can look more at rest? I learned this by trying to take my father's hand one last time. And there was so much make-up. On his hands.

I hadn't held his hand since I was a little girl, but I tried then, and I'm trying now and
holy
fuck
his hand
is moving on its own and I don't --

I take his hand, or really his hand takes mine. He's still not breathing, but I hear the sound of the hospital machines now more than my own racing heart, a series of beeps boiling him down into some numbers and he grips me like someone might grip anything they'll never again let go.

He sits up and probably because I watched too many horror movies growing up and through college, of course the sheet doesn't fall.

Not yet.

And the sheet-shrouded smoke shadow that's definitely my dad turns its stupid, vague head toward me, the nose pointing at me, the gap of a mouth pulling down as it opens.

"Lila, you came," which is the only thing he said to anyone after the fall, before he died.

Of course I did. I never came home for holidays because I always had shit to do and I spent spring and summer breaks with friends at home because I never got to see them and
we always assume we have so much time
so much time.

But time only moves slowly when you're terrified and it's been a long time since I've heard a second hand's tick, but it's during this thought that his second hand cups our hands together and the sheet begins to fall and the ash grey version of my father is in front of me again, eyes aflame with a hot blue arc.

"I miss you every day," I want to say.

"I'm sorry we burned you," I say instead.

He chuckles and I officially don't understand, "Hardly matters to anyone now. What does matter, Lila? What matters?"

And the tears again, and I'm like, "Fuck, Dad, I don't know. I'm really stoned right now and I'm probably being raped by Dudley and I just can't right now."

He puts his second hand to my face and I swear I hear it tick and I can breathe again.

"It doesn't matter where I am now, because I'm always here," he says in a hushed voice to make him sound more reassuring.

And I think about him in this phantom space, draped in smoke, in the otherwise warm grey of my eyelids and I openly fucking weep.

"Here," he points his index finger at my right temple, "and here," he points to two inches above my heart. "Ashes and bones and cherry wood boxes never meant a thing. We have this," and he uses both of his hands, touching those two places to remind me of just what and where.

"Don't compromise yourself, Lila. Especially not for money. I did and I never stopped and I always thought that's why you stopped working with me."

And I'm speechless because I just passed out in the middle of a drug deal.

"You're an artist, Lila. A poet."

His hands fall to his sides and the smoke starts to lift like Karl the Fog in San Francisco and I can't stand it because the dull grey starts to brighten.

I reach out and reach out and grab at nothing and

I'm back in the passenger seat.

Dudley is gone.

I'm expecting to be completely ripped off, no Presence, no money, not even the blunt.

But the phone vibrates a bit, a reminder of an unread text. I look down at myself and see that my clothes don't seem to be rearranged or torn or undone or anything in any way and I'm not sore at all. Actually, I've never felt better.

I take out the shared phone. It's only been a half-hour.

I read the text.

"Amy, my girl. I misjudged you. We were hesitant to bring you in because you just seemed like someone who's never suffered, just wanted a quick buck, but had we known...anyway. Hang on to what's in the trunk. We've got a moving day ahead and it'll just be in the way. Welcome a-fucking-board. If you do good on us this time, who knows what we can do for you?"

There are instructions as to what to do with the car, some dropoff, some bro's name.

I shift in the seat and see the stubbed-out blunt in the car's ashtray.

I slowly get out of the car. I think about my dad.

I head to the back of the car, using the fancy remote to pop the trunk.

Here, and here, and I even point to the places where he'll always be.

But I want to see you, Dad.

I open the trunk and see the imperfect kilo.

I can still see you, can't I?

Just next to it are two duffel bags and now my life is a fucking cartoon. I don't even have to unzip them to know that one is money and the other is drugs.

Part II

Justification

/jəstəfəˈkāSH(ə)n/
noun

An explanation that frees one from fault or blame.

Theory of Just Deserts

Nicole DeGennaro

Well, now she's just getting sloppy," Bernadette said when Lynn came into the kitchen. Lynn, still half-asleep, batted away the proffered issue of *The Journal of Applied Quantum Mechanics* as she made her way to the coffee.

"Too early," Lynn said as she poured herself a large mug, then joined Bernie at the table. "You know I have to start with something simpler, like *Science*." She expected Bernie to smile at her first joke of the morning, no matter how lame. But it didn't even elicit an exasperated eye roll.

"Trust me, you want to read this." Bernie slid the journal across the table, already folded open to a specific article. Lynn sipped her black coffee and scanned the title; when she hit the word *teleportation*, she knew why Bernie had called it to her attention. She flipped through the pages, pausing to examine the figures and diagrams of the teleporter to confirm her suspicions. She didn't need to read the text; it described her machine and her data, although it didn't list her as an author.

"Gillian must know I subscribe to this journal," she said as she closed it and tossed it off to the side in disgust, garnering an arched eyebrow from Bernie. "She's only *pretending* to be clueless, right? Because this is a pretty convincing performance."

"Oscar-worthy, certainly."

"Her name isn't on the article, though. I suppose that shows she still half knows what she's doing." Lynn meant to sound lighthearted, to keep joking about the whole thing, but the words came out clipped, her tone severe. She wrapped both hands around her oversized mug as she repeated the phrase *It doesn't matter* in her head. Instead of having the intended effect, the repetition convinced her that Gillian's latest theft did matter. That it mattered very much indeed.

"Half is being generous, don't you think?" Bernie asked. Lynn heard the words but didn't register them, lost in the swirl of her own thoughts. If it did matter, if she couldn't tolerate Gillian stealing anything else from her, what would she do about it? As with any time she questioned herself or the world around her, she began devising ways to achieve an answer using her best tool: science.

Bernie took one of Lynn's rough russet hands in hers and rubbed the soft skin of her thumb along the scars from metal work and chemical burns that decorated Lynn's knuckles. As a plan began to form in Lynn's head, she squeezed Bernie's hand and met her bright copper eyes. Bernie's brown curls were still untamed from sleep, and they poofed out around her head like a lion's mane. Lynn couldn't help but smile for a moment.

"This is the last time," she said. She pushed aside her half-empty coffee mug, although she didn't remember drinking that much. Then she took Bernie's hand between both of hers; their wedding bands pressed together. "Gillian's name may not be on the article, but mine isn't either, and I have that damn teleporter in my lab *right now*. I built it!" She paused, frowning. "She can't keep doing this to us."

"We *do* still need Gillian's money, though," Bernie said.

"But we don't need her."

Bernie frowned. "What are we going to do?"

Lynn paused and gave Bernie's hand another squeeze. "I think I have a plan. I'm just not sure you'll like it."

"I've never seen you encounter a problem you couldn't solve," Bernie said, holding her gaze steady with Lynn's. "I don't see why this situation with Gillian should be any different. You believe in your abilities, and so do I. So, what are *we* going to do?"

Lynn grinned, then reached over and gave one of Bernie's tight curls a gentle tug. "We're going to invite Gillian to our next experiment."

❧

"I hope you know what you're doing," Gillian said as she walked into Lynn's laboratory, her blond hair as slick as her suit. She reached for an Erlenmeyer flask full of a clear liquid—just water to clean the flask, but with no label Gillian had no way of knowing.

Before she could lift it off the table, Bernie appeared. "Don't touch that." She spirited the flask away, dumping the water down the drain.

"The whole point is that I *don't*," Lynn said in reply to Gillian's statement. She descended a ladder as she finished fine-tuning the particle collider that she had built and used to discover the Higgs boson—and that Gillian had promptly sold the specifications for to CERN. "Not in an absolute sense. Being a scientist is all about admitting your own ignorance of the world and trying to educate yourself—and everyone else, if you're lucky."

"I can respect that; it just seems that most scientists manage to satisfy those requirements without jeopardizing so much." Gillian continued to move around the lab, looking at sealed petri dishes with Bernie's biological experiments still in progress or flasks with chemical concoctions still simmering. But with Bernie hovering nearby, she kept her hands to herself.

"That's because they're not thinking large enough," Lynn said. "They let fear stop them from really exploring what they don't know. They don't even go from point A to B to C. They go from A version one to A version two. Not even a baby step; a shuffle. What they do manage to achieve is negligible—barely a ripple in a bucket."

She walked across the open space of her lab to the machine she had created so she could run experiments on the Higgs field. The large cylindrical disruptor had a control panel across the back end, and its tapered point was currently directed at a six-foot-by-six-foot double-paned glass room laced with wires and sensors. Lynn wanted to record every possible parameter that could be measured so she wouldn't have to repeat her experiment.

"But even ripples can revolutionize a field; they can serve as a starting point for someone else," Gillian said. Lynn and Bernie exchanged an eye roll behind her back at the word "revolutionize"—if scientific revolutions happened as often as she used the word, everyone would be knee-deep in Nobel Prizes.

When Gillian stopped poking around the laboratory and met Lynn at the Higgs disruptor, Lynn continued going over the maintenance checklist instead of stopping to pay her anymorethanmarginal attention.

"I don't disagree. I just think you need people aiming low and high if you hope to find anything at all. So I aim high," Lynn said, turning on power to the machine.

"Maybe too high."

"If you feel that way," Bernie said, "then why are you funding our research?" She came up next to Lynn and began evaluating the readouts from the machine's resting state, turning knobs to adjust the settings. They worked around each other in an elaborate but effortless dance as they prepared the Higgs disruptor for the experiment. Lynn glanced over and smiled, resisting the urge to tug one of Bernie's curls, which were currently held at bay by a thick, tight headband. Bernie had helped with so many experiments over the years that Lynn no longer had to tell her what needed doing. She knew it all almost as well as Lynn, and nothing was more invaluable during an experiment than a competent coworker.

"Because, like you both, my curiosity outweighs my fear," Gillian replied. But even if that were true, their similarities ended there. While Gillian might appreciate science and have a better than average understanding of it, at heart she was an entrepreneur. She sold her knowledge of Lynn's experiments to the highest bidders, no doubt making her investment money and then some back on government and private contracts that Lynn had never wanted to pursue. Although Gillian had never outlined her schemes, her greed had laid them bare.

Lynn didn't mind the greed, although she didn't understand it, either. The corollary of all her conversations with Gillian, but the one aspect they never quite got around to discussing, was how to use the knowledge gained by Lynn's experiments. Where Gillian saw monetary gain—apparently "revolutionizing" a field was a lucrative endeavor—Lynn saw only a way forward, doors opening to the rest of the universe. And it was never a choice for her. When a door opened, she went through it, moved on to the next unknown.

However, she did mind being denied recognition for her discoveries—something Gillian ensured by omitting Lynn's name from publications and outside discussions.

"I think we're good," Bernie said after adjusting one last knob. Lynn grinned and pulled down on a heavy lever; the machine slid forward on a set of rails until the tapered end fit snugly into a hole in one side of the glass room. When she turned around on the platform, she collided with

Gillian, who had been watching over her shoulder. Not for the first time, Lynn caught a hint of satisfaction on Gillian's face, as if she were executing a successful long con. If Lynn hadn't seen it before, she would have thought it imagined because in half a second Gillian's expression had returned to one of detachment: an investor's interest in something she valued but did not understand.

Lynn gave her a wide, friendly smile and sidled away.

"I think it's best if you watch from the observation room. It's—"

"Impervious to almost everything, safer—yeah, I know," Gillian said, cutting Lynn off. "It's also boring. Keeps me away from the action."

With no sympathy, Lynn motioned to the stairway on the left wall, which led up to a room with shatterproof windows that provided an overhead view of nearly the entire lab. After one more appraising look over the disruptor, Gillian headed for the safety of the reinforced steel observation room like a petulant child, dragging her feet the whole way.

Bernie watched Gillian retreat and then caught Lynn's eye, giving her a wink. Gillian could never manage to stay in the observation room for the duration of an experiment, masking her spying and mental note-taking as uncontrollable enthusiasm. But they always made her retreat there to have a brief reprieve from her presence. Lynn suppressed a chuckle.

"I'll go get Pavlov," Bernie said, then made her way to a door underneath the observation room. Gillian pressed her pale face against the room's window to try and watch where Bernie went, but the door rested in the room's one blind spot. Lynn smirked; Gillian thought anything Lynn wanted to keep secret she would hide there. Amateur.

Bernie emerged from the room holding a brown tabby cat. A svelte sixteen pounds, the cat sat resigned in her arms and didn't struggle. Bernie petted Pavlov with one hand while she held him close with the other.

"I know you warned me not to get attached, but I'm attached," Bernie said when she and Pavlov rejoined Lynn, who reached into her lab coat pocket and pulled out a collar. This too was laced with wires and sensors, although Lynn had left the bell attached and unaltered as a bit of a joke.

"I think your parents told you the same thing when you met me, didn't they?" Lynn said, as she latched the collar around Pavlov's neck.

He barely shifted in Bernie's arms and continued staring across the room, ignoring them both in true cat fashion.

"So you told me not to get attached knowing full well I would."

"He's going to survive, so surprise! We have a pet cat."

"I hope that's the only surprise today," Bernie said. Lynn took Pavlov from her and went to the glass room. She slid open a small door and shoved the cat through. He allowed her to do so without acknowledging her existence in any way.

Lynn slid the door closed and crossed her arms. "I think Pavlov's kind of a jerk. Maybe we won't keep him."

"You can't give a present and then take it back."

"He's rude. He hasn't looked at me once."

"...have you ever met a cat before?"

Lynn rejoined Bernie on the control platform. "I'm just saying, with his life in my hands he could at least feign some interest in me. Get me to like him so I'm invested in his survival."

"Maybe you shouldn't have announced that he's going to survive, then."

"Well I can't tarnish my record of successful experiments out of spite, now can I?"

"So this is a conflict between your ego and your scientific integrity."

"Aren't all things, really?" Lynn turned on the screens above the control panel, which showed the glass room and Pavlov from all angles.

"Stick to science, love. Philosophy doesn't suit you."

"You're sweet; always looking out for me." Lynn leaned over and gave Bernie a kiss. "I think we're ready to start." Bernie nodded and walked across the lab to the right wall, where a panel of breakers and switches waited; green and red lights blinked the status of the circuits. On the disruptor, meter needles hovered in a pleasant middle ground, letting Lynn know everything waited on her.

While Gillian wasted her time trying to look for what she thought would be Lynn's hiding spots, the real crown jewel of all Lynn's inventions sat plain as day in front of her and under Bernie's control. Lynn wasn't gauche enough to have a large red button, but one of the switches in the wall panel, as innocuous as the others, controlled the universal backup system she had developed. A hard reset—essentially a time travel device for the entire universe, to send it back in time a few minutes or days. Maybe years, if she reworked the program. She had tested a version isolated on her lab and knew that she and Bernie would maintain their memory of what happened before the reset, which would prevent them from becoming trapped in some kind of failure loop. Everyone else would remain oblivious.

At any sign that something got out of hand with the experiment, Bernie would activate the backup. Although Lynn operated the disruptor, Bernie played the most crucial role—she ensured the safety of the universe.

Lynn looked at the monitors and machine output one more time to confirm that all parameters remained optimal. The disruptor's tapered end pointed at Pavlov, and it hummed as it awaited input. Pavlov began to bathe himself.

"All right; I'm going to start with ten percent Higgs field disruption." Lynn typed in the command, and after a five-second fail-safe delay, one of the readouts blipped. Otherwise, the machine gave no hint that it had done anything—no theatrical laser beams at the cat, no whining noises, not even a louder humming. Pavlov stopped bathing and sat alert. Then he began to float around the glass room.

Lynn smirked.

"Upping to fifty percent."

The machine stayed focused on the floating cat, thanks to some complicated programming Lynn had designed to avoid the human error of trying to lock in on a moving target. Once again she put in the command, and after the waiting period the machine obeyed. This time a few of the meters ticked upward along with the readout blip before everything returned to the optimal settings. Pavlov looked surprisingly unperturbed as he began to move around the room faster.

"Unbelievable!" Gillian said, and Lynn spun around to find her out of the safe room and standing at the base of the staircase, eyes wide as she looked at the monitors. Bernie was already at Gillian's elbow, trying to push her back up the stairs.

"—completely disruptive," Bernie was muttering as Lynn jumped down from the platform and met them across the laboratory.

"I have to see it up close; you have to tell me how you've done this! Do you realize you've just revolutionized space travel? And God knows what else. Everything!" Gillian babbled. Lynn tried to block her view of the machine.

"Gillian, please; I'll explain it all to you once the experiment's complete. I haven't revolutionized anything if we can't finish testing it. Do you understand?" Lynn asked. She exchanged a glance with Bernie, and in that moment Gillian moved past them both and headed toward the machine.

"I need you at the kill switch, Bee. I'll handle her," Lynn said to Bernie as she went after Gillian, who had arrived at the control panel. But, seeming to remember Bernie's earlier admonishment, she did not touch anything. She spun back around to face Lynn, blocking her access to every switch and readout on the machine.

"But disrupting an object's interaction with the Higgs field should affect its mass—why is the cat floating after ten and fifty percent disruption?" Gillian asked, confirming so many of Lynn's suspicions in one question, and she knew then that everything about the experiment had been the correct choice on her part.

"I call the machine a disruptor but it does more than that; it also induces acceleration to prove that it has successfully altered the mass of the object being tested." She paused, thoughtful. "I suppose I could have built a second machine to do the nudging, but that seemed unnecessary when I could make one machine that does—"

"Honey, you're bragging again," Bernie called from across the room.

"Right. I guess now isn't the time for that, as much as I'd love to continue," Lynn said. "So now that you know, will you please step asi— DON'T TOUCH THAT!"

But Gillian had leaned against the control panel, hitting just about every button and lever she could. Whatever input she had given the machine, by the time Lynn shoved her out of the way the command had gone through. The meters' needles flew all the way to the red as the machine began to vibrate. Pavlov, floating around the glass room, hissed. The disruptor began to smoke, and the cat disappeared.

"Did she just kill my cat?" Bernie asked. Lynn tried to power down the machine, but it was preparing to execute another command. With nothing in the glass room to focus on, it started pivoting on its base, shattering the walls.

"You did this on purpose," Lynn yelled at Gillian over the hissing pistons and grinding gears that turned the disruptor. Gillian, sprawled on the floor where she had fallen after being shoved aside, stared in horror at the malfunctioning machine. "You overrode the power down command—that shouldn't be possible!"

"Why would I do that?" Gillian asked. "It's my investment. I want it to work!"

The disruptor stopped pivoting, now facing a cage of lab mice—the next warm-blooded target it had sighted. With any other experiment failure, Lynn would have considered cutting power to the lab, although that would ruin so many experiments in one go and likely fry all the active machinery. In this instance, however, she had a different plan.

"I know you do," Lynn said, stepping down from the platform as the disruptor turned her lab mice into light particles racing around the room with Pavlov. The machine continued its search for more targets. Lynn knelt down next to Gillian, bringing her face close so she could whisper. "You just don't want to credit me for my work, for all I've accomplished. How many of my experiments and machines have you sold to the highest bidder, all while cutting me out of the loop?"

She stared Gillian in the eyes and watched her façade drop, saw the intelligence she knew Gillian possessed finally glimmer through.

"How long have you known?" she asked.

Lynn smiled. "From the beginning. You're too smart to play dumb convincingly."

"If you've known all this time, why does it matter now?"

"Because now I have the means to act."

Lynn stood up and met Bernie's eyes across the room.

"What are you going to do?" Gillian asked, beginning to climb to her feet. Lynn nodded at Bernie, then turned to Gillian.

"I'm going to start over."

Bernie hit the universal backup switch, and Gillian vanished. The disruptor stood inactive, facing the intact glass room. The mice reappeared unharmed. Lynn turned to Bernie, who remained near the breaker panel and looked around as if she wanted to expect an explosion but knew there wouldn't be one.

"It worked," Bernie said, lowering her hand from where it hovered over the switch she had activated about fifteen minutes into a different future, which had sent them back to now, before anything had happened.

"Of course it worked." Lynn walked over and embraced Bernie, who was shaking. "You knew everything would be fine. We went over it all. Even how the machine would look out of control if any button was pushed after the second input completed."

"I wasn't worried about that. I was worried about the universal backup. And, you know, the butterfly effect or something."

Lynn had hypothesized that with careful programming, she could alter some details of the universe without causing a catastrophe, but she hadn't tested that hypothesis. She respected the system and herself too much; the universe didn't deserve to be reset out of a lack of self-confidence. But the situation with Gillian had given Lynn a perfect opportunity—and test subject.

"So you don't actually believe in my abilities, is what you're saying," Lynn said.

"Well, clearly you don't either; you're the one who invented the backup system."

"You know what they say: better safe than dead."

"Nobody says that," Bernie said. Then she laughed.

"What?"

"I can't believe you just pulled off two major experiments successfully. So your Higgs disruptor works, and so does your universal backup. Congratulations."

"I don't know why you're surprised. I've always been ambitious."

They kissed, still embracing, and then stood in silence for a few minutes, the various machines in the laboratory all humming around them. This universe without Gillian Walsh—with no memory of her ever existing, except for in Lynn and Bernie's minds—already seemed happier, brighter.

"You know," Lynn said as a thought struck her, and she and Bernie separated. "I still can't believe you let me erase Gillian from the universe. I thought you were supposed to be my moral compass."

"That doesn't sound like me."

"That sounds exactly like you." Lynn reached over and gave one of Bernie's curls a playful tug. "I'm pretty sure it was in your wedding vows."

"Well, I never promised I'd be reliable, now did I?" After a pause, Bernie shrugged. "The way I see it, we just did the universe a huge favor."

"I'm glad you agree with me," Lynn said, grinning. Bernie glanced across the laboratory as something caught her attention. She took a few steps forward to get a better view, and then she turned back to Lynn, hands on her hips.

"You just couldn't resist, could you?"

In one corner of the lab sat a display case that hadn't existed in the Gillian-infested universe. It held a Nobel Prize in physics for Lynn and one in medicine for Bernie, among other prestigious accolades.

"You said it yourself that we did the universe a favor. I just thought we deserved some recognition. But of course nobody else knows what we did, so I found other ways for the universe to thank us," Lynn said. Bernie rolled her eyes but smiled.

"I got you something else, too," Lynn continued as she crossed the laboratory.

"You mean aside from the now nonexistent Gillian's buckets of money?"

"That is earmarked for research purposes, and you know it!" Lynn disappeared through the door underneath the observation room. A moment later she emerged holding Pavlov.

"Surprise! We have a pet cat."

Good-bye to Nothing

Christopher Rogers

Not even my tinnitus rings here. I've been in sensory deprivation chambers before—that anonymous floating, the gentle water, the deep black—but it's never felt this seamless. A main difference here is that I do not feel in control or at all relaxed. Perhaps if I had the usual comforts from my time in there of noticing my shoulders or legs relaxing, or if I could rediscover a hand or a wrist, but the panic I'm feeling isn't from not being able to move my body or any lack of input from my senses.

Am I in a coma, a sort of prison in one's own mind? Again I say perhaps, but how does one get locked away like that? If I can't remember how, then maybe I can remember why I've been sent here—and that is the sense of it, isn't it? Sent here. The more parts that elude me; I can't even begin to imagine the reason. Key happenings—whether they be the closeness or distance of a loved one, the first time one remembers shedding tears outside of physical pain or things we feel are unfair done to us by one's parents, or the yearning moments before finally seeing someone or being able to do something or realizing one never can—guide you, shape you for the rest of your life. Our core beliefs come from here, it would be fair to say. I started to notice something was wrong when I could no longer clearly remember my seventh birthday, even though I can surmise it's the night my mother left us because she isn't in memories afterwards, however fleeting. I wish we could have said good-bye to her. Our father raised us, and that wasn't so bad, I think, but now that I'm missing another cornerstone I'm beginning to wonder: if I can't recall my first day of high school, which I remember being excited about, was it just a lackluster day, or is something else at play here?

Separated from my confidence, I can't push too deeply all at once; my own mental ground feels unstable, thin as a sheet. Without anchors on my timeline, I suppose I could be anywhere, anyone, anytime. There's freedom in that, but distress in terms of to whom all of the ineffable, effervescent emotions belong.

Discarded; severance, like orphaned tree branches before the trunk is ground to nothing; a fading out before sleep only seen with surrounding haze during recollection. A foreboding sense pervades this place that I may not be in a place at all. Dreams have never felt this clear, not even my most lucid.

A spark of something flicks itself in the back of my mind. It feels like the rush and sudden ache of cleverness. Cleverness fits in my mental hands well. It was my shield and under it I was always sure I crossed every T. Much of my adult life was spent using cleverness to steal credit from two of the most genius minds I knew. Obsessions are common undoings for us all, I imagine; hero or villain, savior or usurper, guardian or thief, we all succumb to troubles and fixations of the mind. I loved them, but the money for their ideas was too good, the attention was too exciting. Loving them wasn't enough. A twinge of regret and longing pinches more than I would've liked. An itch begins where my fingers might be, then in my toes, my knees, my elbows.

Not in a way that's cheesy like a sparkler, but indeed a green sort of fire painlessly bursts through what might have been my body at its larger joints; the bends of my elbows, knees, wrists, shoulders, and hips are all alight. Is my body being torn apart? Did my body even exist before now? Bright as it is near what might be my body's seams, the strange flames don't reach very far into the black. I suppose I'm grateful for them as I am reacquainted not only with these burning parts of myself, but my eyes as well, all sort of confirming that I'm still here. For the moment, I'm still here.

Am I the dream, the dreamer, or simply reliving what was dreamt? I suppose I could be nowhere, no one, never. A fragment, a spark of inspiration, the impetus, that gut feeling you should trust that something is wrong? How old was I? No—am I? How old am I? Think: when was my last birthday, and if I can't remember that, who was there? Who was there might shed some light on when since I never seemed to keep friends for long. All I can find are blank faces, suggestions of bodies, blurs where loved ones used to be. How many are there? I can only see them in mental periphery, but I can count more than twenty before the fog of my memory takes over, and both the number and the fog are comforting. My mental extremities tingle from reaching. Who are they, though? Do you they want to be there?

This dizzying mental dance affirms something in me and for the first time since I started drifting in this endlessness of black and anguish I have the impetus to laugh at myself. Who else in a similar situation would desperately try to confirm that they were popular? I'm thankful that there is an acknowledgement of me, even if it is only from me, but there is also a mix of comfort and despair that Hell might be real after all. Am I on my way to the eponymous God? Are there demon lords here that will revel in my creatively drawn-out destruction?

I suppose that means that I've done something very wrong. Perhaps the wrong was assuming I could out-think two much more gifted thinkers with avoidance and denial. Is this what it's like to be erased? Am I casually being deleted? Click-and-drag-and-empty. Is it vicious, like revenge? It feels like it must be, best served dark and empty until one's body falls apart. Wouldn't it be something if it were an accident?

But I wouldn't have trusted them if I thought they could be so careless. They would be very precise. They would do this. They should. Should have? The same warning ache rises in me and it feels right to think that they've done this somehow. I wish I could've spoken to them before, but to say what? I'm sorry? I am. Maybe all that would remain would be to say good-bye to them. Perhaps it's wrong to be resentful. I banished them to obscurity in many ways. But it is banishment, isn't it? Many literary characters are banished at the beginning of their journeys. Am I being banished at the end? As a means to an end?

Perhaps there's not much of a point in wondering about why I'm here, either. There still isn't any physical pain or smell as more of my body burns away, like someone is taking a sultry drag from the ends of me. I wish I could reach out to them, send a message to them even if only in the form of a repeated phrase throughout the day or the feeling of a presence that embraces. Come to think of it, I wish I could remember their names. They're on the tip of my proverbial tongue, but I suppose the relevance is lost along with me.

What remain are my pangs and sorrows and grief. The feelings of being lost in a foreign city, too arrogant to have dabbled in the language; waiting at a remote bus stop in a downpour, no lights in sight; holding the phone and begging it to ring; burying, but building. There might be some happiness within me yet, but now it only feels right to touch on agony, and not just for myself.

I had always hoped for something more poetic, like the many worlds concept. If the theory is correct, there are so many versions of me that are still out there, many of them on the same paths, repeating the misgivings and crimes. If the theory holds, then I should see—

Green flames in the distance.

Are they also me? Have they seen me? Just as my burning body comforted me, is it comforting to know that many of us have failed in the same way? I suppose it's exciting that the same revenge has succeeded in at least three dozen worlds. What are the odds? Over three dozen of me burning noiselessly in the dark. Are we feeling the same? I wish I could reach out to them, but I'm sure there are rules against that.

We seem to be going somewhere. Are we able to say good-bye? It appeared as a glint at first, a pinhole. Slowly we're being funnelled into now a window of growing, stereotypical white light. I hope that's not what I think it is. I'm not ready for a reckoning, a punishment beyond this punishment. I feel like I've already learned and lost so much. If I could return to how I was, return to those I've wronged and undo it all, I know that I would and never repeat those mistakes. There are likely worlds within which I can and have. Perhaps all that can be done is to lean heavily on the idea that other selves of mine have already made these bold and beautiful choices to stay honest and loyal and worthy.

All of the green flames on me have diminished. Good-bye to my body, I suppose; I don't believe any of it remains. Maybe that's why things seem to be accelerating. As I'm drawn closer to the window or the window is drawn closer to me, I see something of a warm red, like simulated blood vessels, the color temperature of embarrassed skin. Where my heart might have been is the source of what's pulling the window and myself closer to one another, yearning and longing made into a force of attraction. It feels like going home after a very, very long time away.

I can only wonder what will become of the feelings that remain with me. Will they matter? Are experience, compassion, remorse, love, despair, et al, as easily erased? If they can't come with me, will they go anywhere? Will they become part of something new, like the million years of memory humans have in their DNA that can only be crookedly accessed in times of dire need to survive, to persist? Will anyone recognize them as something other than universal? I'm beginning to understand the fascination with pseudosciences and the poetry of star signs. I'm beginning to understand visions, past life regressions, the chasing of ghosts and legends.

What I was really hoping for was illumination, not just of my discarded body as it burned, but the answers to the mysteries I and we have accumulated through our efforts to understand. All of that noise, those plays for power, the supposed high road of being a better person, for what? To reach the end and be greeted with silence—no rapture, no joy, no confrontation of souls—it could never be bitterer. The only answer in the end is another mystery. I somehow want to share it.

I'd love to find my mother and father, together or apart, and just whisper this nothing to them, but what torture would it be to not be able to prepare yourself let alone your beloved child for nothing.

Likewise, I'd love to return and tell those who sent me here what it really is. They must not have known.

I ache to try to think of anything now. The ends of my mind are burning with fatigue and slowly things drift ahead of me. Like running water, I feel the remaining wealth of feeling rush forward.

Along with those feelings, a few more of us go into the window, now a door.

Who am I talking to?
Who will we become?

Good-bye
to nothing.
My turn now
through the
white door.

Good-bye to Nothing

Somewhere.
Someone.
Sometime.

I
inhale
and I
wail.

Just Dessert

Christine Ricketts

It wasn't that Johnny necessarily *meant* to ruin everything. Of that Erik was sure. Reasonably sure. After all, it's just that every little boy liked sweets. That's all it was. Erik was certain that if the cheerful, smiley, useless little brat could actually comprehend anything beyond his own tiny body's persistent craving for sugar he would be deeply ashamed of his actions and would immediately change his behavior. Certainly he would.

Of course, that didn't exactly help Erik at the moment as he circled around his candy shop, searching out the half-eaten bits and pieces that the darling little Johnny always left in his wake. He gathered up chocolate wrappers, picked up chunks of toffee smashed and flung to the floor, and wiped smudgy prints off of glass jars filled with colorful wrappers. Erik frowned as he vigorously rubbed at something that looked almost like blood caked onto the clear surface. Really, the things children put their hands into—

He suddenly stopped still in front of a small display of individual chocolate and fruit pies, each one with a chubby, finger-sized hole in it. Each one of the twelve delicate pastries that he had spent all morning baking. . .

Erik felt his hand clench around a fistful of empty wrappers, which quietly crinkled their protest.

This . . . this could not continue.

Muttering under his breath, Erik stalked over to the counter and shoved up the hutch that separated customer from proprietor. Or, more poetically, savage beasts from simple shopkeeper.

He caught sight of himself in the long mirror that stretched along the wall. No, he thought, that was unnecessarily dramatic. Some of the children that ducked in and out of the shop every day were delightful, happy to exchange slightly sweaty bills for sweets that they enjoyed once they were outside. Only one of them was not like the others. One measly little annoyance doing his best to mess up every carefully structured sugary concoction.

Erik tossed the wrappers into a garbage can tucked neatly away underneath the wide, glossy wooden bar and started forward again. As he passed the polished copper cash register, antique drawer closed and locked, he scooped up the carefully counted day's earnings and continued through the discreet door that seemed to disappear into the wall.

Behind the door a short flight of stairs took him up into small living quarters. Just one room, it held his bed, a desk and a tiny stove with only one burner. The shop itself was three times as large and did well enough that he could more than afford to live somewhere larger with a great deal more luxuries.

But Erik quite liked the simple space; it reminded him of his roots. He was surrounded by towering stone and steel rather than a thick forest, but times change. Times change . . . nobody wanted candy from a moving vehicle, apparently, no matter how charming a covered wagon might be.

He set the money down on the desk and pulled out its chair, sinking down onto the seat. Tipping backwards, his eyes were drawn to the portrait hanging near the stove; an oil painting of an old woman, her nose crooked, her eyes black and beady, and her grey hair pulled back tight in a bun.

"Ah grandmama, how much easier things were in your days! You just tucked the meddlesome children into an oven and served them with honeyed milk. Nowadays everyone is up in arms if you so much as take a grubby finger off of one of the irksome beasts."

The painting on the wall was silent; after all, paintings don't talk. And still, Erik heard everything that it said.

Nothing better as a deterrent. Do you know how many children I had trying to eat their way through my front door? One little scamp bit near down to the hinges!

He nodded his agreement; he often had the sense that the kids visiting his shop were moments away from gnawing at the foundations.

There were a few drawbacks. Not many recipes call for the little darlings and you can only have stew so many times, especially in the summer. All those little bones get stuck in your teeth.

It almost seemed as if the picture was bobbing its head but without any part of it actually moving.

It can backfire on you if you aren't careful. Such an embarrassment to end up in your own oven. They never let me live that one down.

Erik was only half listening. The other half of his attention had stopped at the mention of recipes, turned on its metaphoric heel, and, with a firm nudge, directed his eyes toward the bookshelf that took up the entire left wall of the room.

It was not the kind of bookshelf one would normally find in a home. Sure, there were books and shelves but that was where any remote similarity ended.

For one thing, the books lining the shelves had never been sold in a bookstore, or online, or even out of the trunk of an old beat-up car. Their resemblance pretty much stopped once you got to one of the thick, often horrifyingly decorated covers. There were words printed inside, as well as some pictures, but not any that one would ever want to read or look at directly.

When his eyes finally settled over the particular "book" that he had been thinking of, Erik pushed himself up from the chair, reaching the shelf in two long strides. He tugged the tome down—it was bound in a fuzzy, off-red, semi-cloth-like material—and flipped it open to the part that would, in a normal-like book, contain the table of contents.

This book did not contain a table of contents. It won't be described, in any kind of detail, what it did contain because such horrors are of the type much better left unsaid. In a very loose sense though, it held a wide variety of spells and recipes, some that dealt with people, some that handled food and a few that contained both.

He skimmed a thin finger over the page, careful to keep at least an inch of space between skin and parchment, until he came across a twisting, spidery, word-like creation that made his lips twitch back into the closest approximation of a smile that he could manage.

It looked a bit like that expression that people in old paintings are usually making—like they've just eaten something that they're not sure is agreeing with them.

❦

When young Johnny appeared the next day, it was as if it were any other visit. The little boy waited outside the shop door, his hands tucked into the pockets of his neatly pressed pants. And, as usual, when Erik unlocked the door and pulled it open, Johnny ducked inside with a beaming, if somewhat sheepish, carefully practiced smile. He removed his hands from his pockets and lifted one up in Erik's direction. Clutched in the slightly wet palm were a small number of bills, hastily counted out by Johnny's mother who seemed to find it less stressful to merely keep track of the damages her child made rather than attempt to prevent him from accruing them.

"Here Mr. Erik. This is for the candy I took yesterday. My mom said that I should say, 'I'm sorry for taking them without paying. I promise I won't do it again. I'll look with my eyes and not my hands,'" he recited in the same sing-song voice that he always did. It was full of enthusiasm, sincerity and completely devoid of honesty.

Erik, as he always did, took the damp currency and tucked it into one of his own pockets. And then he did something that he never had done before; he bent over so that he was eye level with the boy and chuckled lightly.

"It's quite important that you do, Johnny. Today more than ever. But I doubt for a second that you will."

The boy, who had frowned at the unfamiliar cackle, tipped his head to one side. "Whatdya mean? Whatdya mean I won't?" A sliver of churlishness crept into his voice, easily knocking aside the previous sweetness.

Straightening, Erik brushed his hands over his shirt front, as if flicking off invisible dust. "Oh, just what I do. I think you won't be able to resist touching the candy. After all, you never have before, right?"

Johnny's face scrunched as he considered the words. He was used to adults falling for his smile. This sounded different. "Is this like . . . like a *dare*?"

Erik tipped his head in cheerful mimicry of the boy. "If you'd like."

"What do I get if I win?"

"Any piece of candy in the store."

68

Johnny thought very hard and very fast. Truthfully he didn't really even like candy; it was gritty and too sweet and got stuck in his teeth. But he did like dares and he did like to win—he figured that it was only a few minutes of playing nice. And if he got bored with it, well, there was no reason he had to *keep* playing nice.

"Okay!" he agreed, clasping his hands very obviously behind his back. Perhaps if he had thought a little harder and little less fast, Johnny would have wondered what would happen if he *didn't* win but then that would have meant that the idea had even occurred to him.

Still smiling, Erik held out one of his hands. Johnny stared at it, chewing thoughtlessly on his bottom lip before bringing one of his own hands out from behind his back. They shook briefly and Johnny immediately tucked his hand away again.

Erik stepped over to the counter and left the boy to his own willpower.

Johnny began his circuit of the shop as he always did; at the far wall where tall glass containers of brightly colored taffy and hard candy were piled atop each other. Those were easy enough for him to resist; they hurt his teeth since he rarely had the patience to let them sit on his tongue. They'd crack when he threw them on the floor and stepped on them but the wrappers kept the pieces from flying everywhere.

He moved on to the wooden bins filled with caramels and gummies. His fingers twitched as they clasped each other out of sight; he liked to smush the fruity candies between his thumb and forefingers. If he dropped them to the ground he could smash them even more without anyone even noticing.

Erik, who tracked the boy's movement in the mirrored wall, saw the first real hints of struggle play across the cherub cheeks as Johnny wound his way through the display tables clustered near the center of the store, laid fresh with new hand-sized pastries baked that morning. *No doubt imagining sticking his plump little fingers into each and every one of them,* Erik thought, a hint of sourness cutting through the otherwise gleeful feelings that were turning about his brain.

He was somewhat correct; the real thought went something more like throwing the puffed shells down onto the floor and stomping on them until the gooey or creamy insides squirted out.

Still, Johnny did neither of those things. He just continued to wander slowly about, his hands never shifting from their station. And though his nose sometimes came precariously close to a dollop of frosting or jam, it never actually touched.

But Erik wasn't worried and not just because these types of deals always have a backup loop. He turned around at the counter just as Johnny reached the last section of the shop, stocked floor to ceiling with chocolates; this part he did not want to watch secondhand in a mirror.

Johnny loved chocolate; not the way it tasted, but the way it shattered into countless little pieces. He always saved this section of the store for last and it was where he did most of his damage. But this time he kept his hands neatly tucked away as he roamed through each display.

Until he lifted his head to follow the line of one particular setup, carefully constructed that very morning. Two rows of brightly colored boxes, tied with pretty ribbon, were stacked atop each other like two staircases rising up towards . . .

A two-foot-tall statue of a little boy made out of chocolate. It had its hands placed on its hips and looked so life-like that Johnny thought for a moment that it would jump down from the table and run out the shop door.

The only thing missing from the sculpture was a face; where there should have been a face carved into the sweet, shiny surface, it was just blank, non-expressive chocolate.

His fingers itched. He wondered if he pushed the statue or bumped the table, would it fall to the floor and explode into a million delicious pieces? Was it just a hollow shell? Or was it all a solid piece? Would his teeth hurt if he tried to bite through it? What if he left it out in the sun? Would it melt into a puddle on the sidewalk?

I'm melting! I'm melting! He could already hear the cries in his head and grinned.

"How come it doesn't have a face?" he asked, without turning to see where Erik was. He gave a little start of surprise when the shopkeeper appeared next to the chocolate figure.

"I didn't think it needed one," Erik said with a shrug.

Johnny pouted his lips and continued to stare. It ought to have a face, he thought to himself, his fingers tapping against each other unnoticed. I could give it one . . .

"That's the one I want," he declared.

Erik lifted an eyebrow. "Hmm? What do you mean?"

"You said I could have any piece that I wanted. I didn't touch anything so I win. I want this one."

"Oh, I don't think you want this one. It's awfully big don't you think? If you ate all that chocolate, you'd make yourself sick. How about something else?"

Johnny shook his head. "No. I want this one." He could already imagine breaking it in half. Or watching it slowly melt. Or—

"Are you sure? You can have something else if you'd like. Anything else."

Rolling his eyes, Johnny just barely resisted reaching out and grabbing the statue himself. "This one. This is the one I want," he insisted.

Lifting his shoulders with something almost like a sigh, Erik started to reach for the statue, "Well all right then, if you're sure—"

"Wait!"

Erik froze, his hands inches from the molded chocolate. Disappointment started to rise in his throat until he caught sight of the look on Johnny's face. The little boy was staring at it intently with a hunger that Erik couldn't quite describe but that reminded him of some of the books on his shelf.

"I want to taste it before you wrap it up."

Smiling faintly, Erik lowered his hands and stepped backwards. "Of course, of course. Here, I'll trim a bit off the foot for you, shall I?"

Bobbing his head, Johnny shifted back and forth, watching as Erik cut through the small chocolate shoe with a thin blade. It snapped off with a quiet pop and Johnny could see that the piece behind it was thick and solid. It was solid! He'd have to work hard to crush it into pieces. He was already imagining all the tortures he could wreak upon it. He wanted to mash it between his teeth; gnash it like a giant raging beast of terrible—

Bouncing with excitement, he grabbed the piece from Erik's outstretched palm and crammed it into his mouth. The sweet, creamy taste of chocolate exploded over his tongue.

And then the world went dark.

‹ই৵›

71

In the candy shop Erik slipped the knife into the apron tied around his waist. Then he reached out and lifted the chocolate statue from its current display and walked it over to a new one set up just inside the door. He adjusted the stand beneath it until it was just the right height to catch the eye of anyone passing by. Then he surrounded it with candy filled boxes and bags, a treasure hoard of sweets.

And when he had placed the last piece, a plain white card with the words "Free Samples" printed neatly on it, he leaned toward the chocolate center piece, as if he were whispering to it,

"Now you can have whatever piece you'd like, Johnny." Smiling, his lips finally pulling all the way back in a wide grin, Erik stood up and walked to the shop door, propping it open to the noisy sound of passing traffic and the chattering approach of children.

What a wonderful day it was.

The little chocolate statue looked out, its incredibly detailed face caught up in surprise so realistic that it almost seemed that the tiny eyes were whipping back and forth.

Part III

Disambiguation

/dɪsæmˌbɪgjuːˈeɪʃən/
noun

The removal of ambiguity by making something clear.

The Moon Pulls at Us

Christopher Rogers

ll during the journey, from the boat across the Pacific, to the plane across America, then into a van driven by a man whose face was shadowed by a New York Yankees baseball cap, I was naïve and far enough along in English to imagine Kingston to be a town of kings.

It was very late when we were dropped off at our new home; it wasn't a palace, but I think, at the same time, even I was realistic enough at the time to know it wouldn't be. Still, I sunk more than a bit when I saw it was maybe a converted two-story mechanic's garage. We were at the end of a very long driveway and midway between was a large parking lot. Beyond that, I could only see the edge of a formidable building. Perhaps there was a palace here yet, I thought.

Sixteen women living under one roof is difficult enough between the moon's pulling at us and personality clashes, but the isolation in all of the crowding was even stronger. We did not forget gossip or jealousy, but it mattered much less. We only had each other, so it was deeply wounding when we disagreed. Worse than that, we were quickly orphaned from our heritage.

We were brought to America in debt and, to work it out, we are staffed in a Japanese restaurant. Our room and board costs come out of our daily earnings, which aren't meager, but what we receive is because the rest goes to all of the trouble it took to get us into the Land of the Free. At times, I feel as if we will never be free, but I have met the owners of the Peking Duck and they were born in a region neighboring mine. Maybe we could all become owners.

Tsuyoshi isn't Japanese. He doesn't even want to be and maybe that's part of his sadness. I think we'd be doing a little better if, for example, Mountain Flower was not now supposed to be Masako, Bright Shining Future did not have to wear a name tag that said Sakura, The Way the Light Comes In did not become Riku, Admiring Luxuriance was never Murasaki, and I, Wise Jade Tinkling, never became Ai. We learn that shrimp is *ebi*, squid is *ika*, *tamago*, *nori*, *saba*, the difference between *sushi* and *sashimi*, basic phrases for serving the few-and-far-between potential Japanese clients, and Japanese etiquette, how to take the singsong quality out of our speech, and how to be meeker, but we never learn the comfort of what these new names mean. I am also certain there is poetry to them. There has to be.

I struggled at first with the day-in and day-out. I'd never been a part of the service industry, in particular, one that requires its workers to operate as gentle shadows with keen instincts for when anyone behind paper doors in a tatami room needs even the smallest thing. It was tricky to learn how to eat our "free" lunch in the bustling, hot kitchen in under five minutes and not feel nauseous.

Sometimes the kitchen staff would look at us too long, hunched over a table by the dishwasher. We could all feel it, but neither the kitchen staff nor we said a word. Even if they had, we didn't speak their language. Admiring Luxuriance told me, as she and a few of the other girls smoked by one of the open windows in the garage, that she saw Kind and Fragrant at the bottom of the basement stairs. She was leaning over as if she had lost something, like spare change or a contact lens, but Admiring Luxuriance says she withdrew when she saw the sous chef behind her, helping her. He was, of course, also helping himself.

Most of us laugh, and some of us want similar experiences, but we all know how forbidden it is for us to endanger our stay here. To be sent home would not only be a great shame for us, but we would have to pay for our banishment and still have to work out our debt in poor places under poorer conditions. The lure of the supposed needs of the body is great, though. Just as the moon decides our tides, so does our racing heart decide that, yes, there are instincts within us as we yearn not for eventual babies, but closeness and the kind of talk that comes during and after and ever after.

In the time and aches between, we smoke. Each drag is god in substitution. Each drag has a lover inside it and we draw them in more deeply and eagerly the shorter the cigarette burns, knowing that we accelerate the coming of the end and only brevity grows. Each drag holds a key to inner parts of us we can only glimpse for a moment as its generosity comes with a cough, a huskier voice, and a habit that only gets fatter and needier. The routine of it, the dependency on it can make even the hardest moments seem normal, regular.

Regulars are a blessing. Naturally, they tip better, and it's always nice to be requested as a server, but it dispels the pretense. I especially like the ones with babies, even if they cry.

Six months into my working at Suzume, the Tailored Suit asks me in Japanese what my name is. I lower my head and blush, though it is not because I am flattered.

"Ai," I breathily let out. "What is yours?"

He turns his head slightly, like dogs do when the pitch of anything is shrill. "Where are you from?" in English.

I blush again. "Outside of Osaka," in English. And I immediately know it's too specific.

"I travel a lot for business, but I've never heard your dialect. Maybe this is just my trouble with Osakan, though. I didn't quite grasp it. Strangely, hama-kotoba—the Seahorse Speech in Hokkaido—made more sense to me."

I bow and withdraw backwards and quickly. I would love to be found out, I think among many racing thoughts.

He left a note on the back of the check for me, "I didn't mean to embarass you. Tell me your real name next time. I'm just curious." And then what I could only guess to be a translation in very careful Japanese.

I wish I knew his name. He always pays in cash.

Admiring Luxuriance cackles at this, not bothering to stifle it at 02:00. Through smoke at the window, she hushes herself to a fast whisper, "He really likes you. Be careful not to become like Mountain Flower."

I don't have to ask her what she means as the rumor mill turns tirelessly. It had long been suggested that she and a few of her customers were closer than banter allows and some of them had moved on after tension at the table. She was also rarely seen at lights out, but was almost always at breakfast. With all of the intimacy and pleasure she must've been experiencing, though, she seemed sadder and sadder as the days went on.

"Perhaps she and Tsuyoshi have too much in common," I leak into the early morning air, thinking of the dark clouds that follow the two of them. We both silently nod at this. In the silence that follows, maybe we both thought about how there isn't a way out.

Luxuriance grins, forgetting her volume, "But Tailored Suit seems happy. He always comes in with friends and they talk and drink and laugh. Wise Jade, would you ... ?"

I draw heavily on my cigarette and stare up the driveway through the window.

She asks again, but whispering, "I know a lot of these girls want to leave this place. The price of living here and shoving our meals down our throats is so much that the debt will last a long time. Mountain Flower is even being charged interest, like a real loan! Are you looking for a way out with this man?"

I draw even longer on the cigarette and then stub it out and move slowly to bed. She watches as I get into bed, the open room supplying none of us any shield from my tears, the answer to her question.

We all wake just as the sun is rising to the sound of Mountain Flower making a sort of phantom heaving, trying to silently sob. Admiring Luxuriance and The Way the Light are already with her, but no one is using words. As I sleepily get nearer, they shoo me away, but not before I see blood.

"I can help," I said, suddenly too awake, thinking of things I learned working as a doctor's assistant.

"No one can," The Way the Light Comes In says, soberly.

Kind and Fragrant guides me away by the arm and we gather outside with the other girls. We ache while we are numb; we smoke because what else is there to do? An ambulance comes without its sirens and lights on. Tsuyoshi surfaces like a ghost exiting the back door of the restaurant, silent and pale. As briefly as we see him, he disappears into the ambulance with Mountain Flower and we can hear a brief, soft inhale as we all slowly begin to understand.

I help The Way the Light Comes In clean the bed. It spread farther than I thought it would've, but I also thought there would be more to it. I remember seeing Luxuriance move a red mass, but it could've been pooling blood. Memory keeps increasing the size of it, so I try to help clean because I don't feel sick, like the other girls. As the more of the red disappeared, more girls reappeared, asking how they could help as a form of apology. The stain would never be completely gone, but we scrubbed and soaked and blotted and worked ourselves to pruning. Eventually, we started asking:

A glass of water,

a different fitted sheet (the first was for a larger bed),

pull this corner,

open the far window too,

who has a cigarette?

Tsuyoshi came back in time for breakfast at 11:30. We had all made coffee at this point, but waited to eat and sit with him at the communal table. No one spoke and he looked as though he'd aged ten years. No one wanted to ask if she were dead, but we could all feel the question was looming. Eventually, having barely touched his "free" miso soup and rice, he stood.

"She will be home tomorrow, we think."

We opened for lunch as usual.

Bright Shining Future and I always meet between lunch and dinner to smoke outside the back door at as the sun goes down. In the winter, it's my favorite, since the hard-to-look-at blues of twilight unfold before us as we catch up, commiserate, and speculate.

"Do you think the baby was his?" she asks the obvious.

"Do you think she wanted it?" I push back.

"But wasn't she with that guy Vincent a lot?"

"She was? I thought it was Alex again."

"The bald guy from the summer? No way. He got married, moved to Florida."

Our smoke doubles with our breath in the cold and the landscape fades in and out of our chatter.

"Did you see Tailored Suit has a reservation tonight? Party of two."

Two? It's usually at least four. "I didn't."

"Maybe you shouldn't. I can cover it if it's in your section."

"No, I can do it. I'm not..."

"No, of course not."

But am I?

And just as Bright suggested, he arrives, but he is alone. I seat him and he smiles at me, bigger than usual, for longer than usual. I nearly run into the prep kitchen. Is he doing this to hurt me? What will she be like? She probably has a savings account, bigger breasts, and writes English poetry. And her lips probably don't part as strangely, and...

I compose myself, technically stealing a cup of the higher-end tea. I go back to him, but he is still alone.

"Ai. How are you?"

I return the sentiment.

"But really, how are you this evening? Are you all right?"

And I want to breakdown, pour everything out that I'd seen this morning, how I've already been awake fourteen hours, having slept two. About how I lo-

"It's been a rough day, but I am OK. You are alone tonight ...?"

"It's probably very forward of me, but I wondered if you could be my guest."

I take a step back, which is my mistake, I know.

"Sorry, I...I should've guessed. You're working." He starts to gather his overcoat, bag.

"No!" too loudly.

He freezes, "... no?"

"You're half-Japanese, right? That's why you know it so well?"

"Yes, and half Chinese."

A distant cousin of mine is a halfy and no one speaks to her. "Then maybe you will understand why I haven't told you." I drop English, I drop the dead cadence and I tell him who I am.

"Wise Jade Tinkling," he repeats. How can this be?

I say something stupid like, "Yes?"

"That's just perfect. I'm very glad to finally meet you. If you really can't be my guest this evening, then perhaps another evening? I don't want to get you in trouble." He hands me his card.

"Takeshi. What does it mean?"

"Something like, 'Unbending, like a bamboo tree.' But call that number whenever you're ready to meet with me outside of here, Wise Jade Tinkling."

Dinner moves on like normal, he dines alone, tips too generously, and leaves without many more words between us.

"Think about it," he says with a slight bow, then a shy wave over his shoulder as he leaves.

When Mountain Flower returns, we put her straight to bed, which we've surrounded with spare screens for her privacy. She doesn't speak, just stares ahead. We bring her tea and her meals. She doesn't speak, more staring. A few days go by. She only gets up to go to the bathroom, smoke at the window. Still, she doesn't speak, only stares ahead and through us.

A man in a cheap suit comes and meets with Tsuyoshi. The rumor mill turns, but isn't given long. Between lunch and dinner a week after Mountain Flower was sent to the hospital, we are summoned to a meeting at the communal table. The man in the cheap suit is telling us that Tsuyoshi is taking a leave of absence, which we interpret as he is fired. In two days' time, the man in the cheap suit will lead the restaurant. He says his name is Nobunaga, but that night as we close Suzume, I'm mopping near the bottom of the stairs to Tsuyoshi's office when I hear him cry out, dropping English and the flat cadence, "Why? Why would you do this?" And then a couple of wet thuds and silence. A small number of girls join me, but we were only brave enough to linger at the bottom of the staircase. The door opened slowly after a time, and, of course, Mountain Flower walks through it, a knife undoubtedly reddened with Tsuyoshi. She sleepwalks by us and puts it on a tray all by itself in the dishwasher. She closes it and walks away as the hot water scalds his life from the metal.

"What will happen to her now?" Someone murmurs as I notice no one moving to stop her. She leaves through the back door and Bright Shining Future calls the police. It takes them twenty minutes to arrive.

I shouldn't have, but as I watched the black bag—with Tsuyoshi within—being carried out by two barrel-chested men, I put my hands deep into my pockets looking for comfort. I fingered the edges of Takeshi's business card and with it I found a fear of love and all the trouble it is to be vulnerable and authentic and human, the time it gets to know someone.

As my eyes welled up, I breathed the idea of him in and along with all of our possible dreams and eventual babies came the fear of life without them. In the time between now and our closeness and the kind of talk that comes during and after and ever after, I opened my pack of cigarettes to find I only had one more. It would be the last time that I ached and smoked.

By Any Other Name

Christine Ricketts

They call him One Eye. But that is not his name.

He has had many names, some given, others taken. One had once brought thunder when spoken aloud, another has been whispered softer than the way light comes in. His name has tinkled like pieces of jade and swayed like mountain flowers in the wind.

This one is new. It does not wave or boom or flow; it sits, like a stone placed so that it can never tumble. It binds like a rope his neck has never borne. It limits what should have no limit.

They call him One Eye. Excited, chattering minds that are there where previously they had not been. Who they are, he does not know. Where they have come from, he does not know that either.

Why they have come, that is easy enough. Why have they ever come? It draws them in, slumbering so close to the surface. It . . . it . . . what is it? He remembered once, long ago. Or perhaps it had been tomorrow? Or will be? Or has been. The memories are twisted—twisting—together and there is no thread to pull to untangle them.

They call him One Eye. He has a name, a *true* name but he is sure that there are none left that know it. Some days even he is certain he has forgotten it, so cluttered are the confines of his mind. But it is there, swimming beneath the fog of memory.

They call him One Eye.

. . .

He does not like it.

৵ৢৢ৽

They have come to dig at the earth. Four of them, with small spades

85

and wide brushes and other odd tools. They brush away and gently pick at the dirt, inch by inch, as if each bit of soil is precious. Their hands are steady in their work, their heads bent in supplication to the task. Words float between them in quiet tones broken occasionally by a pitched call of excitement. But mostly they are silent in their minor movements.

Mostly they are focused solely on their labors and do not pay him much attention. The initial interest following the discovery of him has faded; they have given him a name. He is no longer unknown to them.

He does not mind. He has long been alone and will be alone again once they are gone.

Surely they will soon be gone.

One of them is different. She speaks at him whenever she spots him nearby, watching her work, and leaves him small bits of food leftover from her meals.

He ignores both the food and the speech, drawing back into the underbrush whenever the words begin.

It does not stop her from speaking them. She simply continues on as if he were sitting beside her. The words are not the ones that he remembers but he understands them nonetheless.

How did you come to be here, One Eye? Murasaki thinks that you might have wiggled your way through some crevice back when you were small.

He has never been small.

Tsuyoshi says that there must have been an opening in the past that collapsed. Perhaps you wandered in one day and then found your way out blocked.

He has never wandered.

Takeshi never says anything; only smokes by himself.

I wonder if maybe you have always been here?

He has always been.

Others appear soon after, four-footed creatures and winged beasts that follow the now-trampled path. They have come to gloat, he is sure of it. Come to see the once mighty fallen low. He does not meet their blinking, curious gazes, and disregards the way they sniff at the air, the way they fill the space that belongs to him.

Until he realizes that they are not like him and not like the beings he once knew. They are just animals; simple, base shells that are void of thought and interested only in an unfamiliar scent. Their attention becomes little more than a need to avoid him.

He finds this somehow worse than their curiosity.

ঌ৵৹ঌ

Each day more and more of the earth is pushed aside and the excited shouts become more frequent. Pieces of the past are being uncovered; he does not see them but he can feel their rise to the surface. Cracked and broken clay once held aloft by chanting voices is pulled from its resting place to once again feel the air upon its surface.

He feels the shift below the earth as well even though they do not and the words spoken to him darken.

Murasaki says that I am acting childish and not at all like a proper research assistant. That I spend too much time in my books and not enough time in the field.

Tsuyoshi says that we cannot all dig in the same space. We must separate further.

Takeshi still says nothing. He smokes so often that Tsuyoshi has told him to go off by himself. I am glad; I hate the smell of his smoke.

How did you get your scar, One Eye?

ঌ৵৹ঌ

He remembers the Time Before and things are very different. Or maybe he does not remember and everything is the same? Either way he feels lost in a place that is well known to him. None of the paths that he walks take him to the same places they once did. Or maybe it is that he has forgotten which paths lead to which places?

He takes one step forward, then backwards, then left, and then right. Each direction pulls at him but none go where he wants to be.

They call him One Eye but that is not his name. He has a name. Where is his name?

He lies down in the center of the path, too afraid to answer.

ঌ৹৵ঌ

They pull a figurine from the earth, small and made of baked mud. Their chatter is non-stop and fevered for a long while afterwards.

The ground trembles motionlessly beneath their feet but nothing

87

derails their speech. All around them the air is changing, but it goes unnoticed. Sly shadows dart between them, tendrils strangely gentle as they brush against faces and throats.

He tries to slink closer, drawn by the echoes of the past; something is calling him. There is something that he is supposed to do. Something he is supposed to be.

The shadows curl away from him.

The one called Tsuyoshi chases him off.

☙◆❧

None of the others can feel it. They see only the ancient pottery and worn statues. Maybe their families have been away for too long. Maybe they have lost the favor they once knew. But my family was the last to leave--our roots had to be torn out. And when you tear a plant out from the ground, some pieces are always left behind. I can feel them.

I can feel you.

❧◆☙

It is nearly dark when they discover the top of the altar. It lists to one side as if it is teetering on some unseen edge deep below the ground. Or maybe it is the world that has shifted. Strangely, the discovery brings no excited shouts or rapid-fire words.

Only more digging.

The shadows are everywhere; they drape across bodies like heavy shawls, squeezing and undulating like serpentine coils.

*Murasaki says I am not to leave the site for any reason; there is too much work to be done. She says this **to me** but it does not seem like she is **speaking to me**.*

Tsuyoshi is pacing back and forth, mumbling under his breath about time, about light, about shadows.

Takeshi says nothing; he has not stopped digging for days.

Tsuyoshi stops his pacing to tell Takeshi he must go slower or else he will damage the structure. But Takeshi acts as if he does not hear him: he wields the shovel like a weapon attacking the earth.

Why are you here, One Eye?

☙◆❧

He hides himself in the underbrush; away from the deepening shadows, away from the quieting words, away from the echoing past.

Something pulls at him but he ignores it. There is nothing for him anymore; he is forgotten. He is an artifact that was never buried in the earth.

He cannot even remember his own name.

⊷⊶

He loses time, wrapped up in the cocooning embrace of bough-filled branches. When he wakes there is blood where there has not been blood before.

On the ground nearby the one called Murasaki is curled up, hands clutching a wound in her side.

Where are you, One Eye!?

The shout comes from both within his mind and outside of it. He is at his feet before he can even think to stand. He pushes out from the branches and rushes toward the only light that is visible.

They call him One Eye; it is not his name.

But it will do.

⊶⊷

The altar is the first thing he sees; it has been completely uncovered. A stream of light from a single lantern falls over it. She is kneeling before it, lips moving soundlessly as if in prayer.

Behind her is the aftermath of an intense struggle. The ground is churned and broken up by footprints and deep impressions—as if something had been thrown repeatedly against the soft earth. Not far away is a body lying still: he cannot see the face but it must be Tsuyoshi because Takeshi is standing only a few feet from her, face nearly obliterated by shadows. The man is motionless but the darkness around him is reaching out towards her, held back by some invisible barrier. But she flinches each time the shadowy fists strike against the unseen wall and the darkness knows that she is weakening.

He lands silently beside her with a growl that is muted but not weightless. The shadows shrink back momentarily but he cannot push them away entirely.

There is a hand upon his shoulder; eyes still tightly closed, she has reached out to clutch at his fur. He can feel her fear and uncertainty as it trembles over her skin.

`Tell them your name.`

89

Ai! My name is Ai!

The shadows whip around her and there is a mocking kind of laughter to the movements.

`Tell them your real name.`

I . . . I don't remember.

`Don't be afraid. I am here. Tell them your real name.`

I can't. They took it from me. They said it wasn't right.

`No one can take our names from us. Tell them. Tell me.`

The shadows crash over each other like storming waves rolling along a beach. They wait, curling and twisting with impatience. The silence stretches until it snaps and they spring forward, tendrils gaping like a great snarling mouth.

He leaps into the air, teeth bared, fur blinding bright even in the darkness.

Words, barely heard, fall from her lips.

≈◈≈

Where there was darkness, there is once again a clearing. Murasaki holds a side no longer red with blood. Takeshi helps Tsuyoshi to his feet.

Above the altar, fading but still visible, is perched a great white wolf, eye wide and unblinking.

Lighting Options

Nicole DeGennaro

The light shifts, and the gateway appears. I step through it onto neon blue sand. Once the disorientation of acquiring a new version of myself fades, I bend down to touch the grains. For a moment I catch sight of my hand and stare at its unfamiliar form. New world, new body. There are three long, delicate protrusions with a near-translucent webbing between them that glitters in the odd light, as if I'm made of gemstones. It can be alarming when your expectations are wiped away and you see everything, even yourself, without any filter. But that is what makes this mode of travel possible.

In this body I have more limbs than usual, all similar fins with spindle-like extensions, and I use them to draw patterns in the velvet sand. It slides back into place when I'm done, behaving more like gel than grains. As I start to glide across it, the viscous substance swallows all signs of my movements. It is nothing like sand; I realize that initial impression was simply my assumptions sneaking back in without my noticing. Nothing would be able to leave a mark on this blue surface.

"Impressive," a voice says, and my head snaps up. I have been in bodies where my thoughts were projected outward, somehow became sound without being uttered. But the part of myself that has always lived here and would recognize its own voice is alarmed. That's how I know something else has spoken.

It takes me a moment to find the other creature; everything shifts with the light when my mind is unhindered by expectations, so I have a hard time distinguishing it from the scenery. The trails of other travelers crisscross in the air, passing through portals I've used or vanishing into ones I cannot yet access. Somewhere between all that, a being like me is standing.

"I've not met another who's collected so many fragments of themselves," it says, but I am stunned by its own collection; the being is fanned out like a deck of cards, a different version of itself peeking out from behind another and another into what may be infinity. Nausea overtakes me, and I have to close my eyes (so many eyes, this strange body on this strange planet). It is a more complete creature than anything I've encountered.

"I have hardly a fraction of myself," I say; it comes out as a gasp as I try to keep down my stomach bile. To cope, I select a form for the other being in my mind. Something to fit this planet: the spindly fins, the gemstone skin. I take a deep breath; when I open my eyes the being before me is one solid creature, its multitude of cards stacked neatly so I am seeing only the one I've picked.

But I still have a keen sense of the depth of the deck, far more robust than my own.

"Ah," it says as it inspects itself; my choice for its appearance has influenced its self-image, I know. In all my journeying, that has been a consistent phenomenon, even among creatures unable to move between realities. Our minds are so easily influenced by outside sources. "Not what I would have picked, but it's certainly fascinating."

I go cold, and it takes a minute for me to realize that the sensation is this body's manifestation of embarrassment. The other being approaches me, and I do not retreat. Perhaps I have unlearned how to be afraid, have permanently shed the internal filter that would lead me to be cautious. Perhaps that shedding is necessary to be as I am.

"How long have you been collecting?" I ask. The creature shrugs; in these bodies, it's a ripple that starts in the center and spreads outward.

"Does time mean anything to you anymore?"

It's right. I can't recall when I last wore a watch or took note of a clock in any reality. I mark the minutes by waiting for the light to shift and reveal a new gateway so I can discover another piece of myself living someplace I have not yet visited. It most often happens for me in a certain type of moonlight, so I keep time by sunsets.

"But I know it has been...quite a while," the being continues. It motions across the expanse of neon blue, moving its spindles in an elegant, comfortable motion. Not at all like the awkward way I navigate this body. "How often does the light from the triple suns reflect just so in a drop of sap? It is a fickle thing, this way of travel."

At once all the hearts of my various acquired selves seize. It is the surge of an emotion that has a multitude of names with the same meaning: kinship discovered. Soulmate found. But with it comes a fallout, a terrible vacuum: the certainty that I am inadequate, too incomplete.

"Is it possible to be complete?" I ask. "Or is this for nothing?"

Its angular face forms odd creases, perhaps indicating surprise, but more likely alarm. It is only a few feet away from me now; I hadn't noticed its continued approach. It closes the remaining distance by embracing me with a few of its graceful limbs.

"I don't think it is possible to be complete; can't you feel how infinite the universe truly is?" it whispers, still holding me close. It must know this truth will drive a desperate hopelessness through my entire being, reaching even the parts I haven't collected yet. Its words have transformed me into a conduit transmitting a devastating message to unknown reaches of spacetime.

When it releases me from its embrace, I almost sink into the slick surface upon which we balance.

"But does this feel like nothing to you? Does it feel unimportant?" it asks.

"I...I don't know." But I do. I live every moment yearning for the gates. It's not that I think my life depends on visiting these other places—in fact, I'm certain I'd be alive either way. But I wouldn't *feel* alive, and there's a bigger difference between being and feeling than between my reality and this one with the neon surface.

Seeking completeness is the only thing that *does* matter. The only task of any importance.

"You know much more than you admit to yourself. That is another reason we explore the universe. You collect your missing fragments, but you also find that you had some of them already and weren't aware."

The hopelessness evaporates, at least for the moment. It sends a final tingle through me, then dissipates like mist during sunrise. I don't know if it's this new version of myself or something about my fellow collector that has elicited so many emotions, but I find the tumult is not unpleasant—disconcerting, but welcome.

As I have searched for the scattered cards from my deck, I have lost other things. Companionship. Connection. Permanence. I didn't think I minded, but facing this being now, I wonder if what I've gained is worth what I've sacrificed.

"Don't go," I say, although it has made no move to depart.

"I think you mean: let's go. Together." It holds out just one spindle, a gentle gesture—a suggestion rather than a command.

I don't hesitate; I am worried any second of doubt or delay might demolish the fragile emotional structure being built between us. My gesture is not half as graceful, but our spindles hook. Our journey begins.

It leads, and relinquishing control leaves me lightheaded. The only way to see the portals and travel through them is to be constantly alert. If the light shifts your way and you're too busy seeing what you expect, you'll miss your chance. The brain fills information in based on what it thinks it knows—not just for blind spots in fields of vision, but for anything. To traverse spacetime as I do is to resist that subconscious process. Managing your perceptions is the skeleton key that unlocks the universe.

When I'm journeying alone, I'm the only one with that key, so I can never let my attention lapse. But with a companion, I can hand off control. It is more liberating than I expected—ultimate freedom multiplied.

The other being leads me back the way it came. We pass through a portal and enter a town of kings. Gilded buildings glitter in the sunlight. The trees are oozing a fragrant burgundy resin. Everything is finely rendered, even the beings of this world—like sculptures instead of actual objects and creatures. Yet it all hums with vitality.

"This is your home?" I ask. Our decks have shuffled, and we are each in a form better suited to our regal surroundings. We are elegant angles and curved horns, vibrant colors and fluid movements.

"Are not all these realities our home?" it replies. For simplicity, I have always considered moving through the portals to be space travel, but I've never been certain these places are separate from each other or different shades of the same reality. I suppose the difference between those two ideas can once again be reduced to a matter of perception. Given that a version of myself has existed everywhere I have been, alternate realities seem more likely, which would make all these places a type of home.

"But this is not where I spend my idle moments," it continues—I had been too busy daydreaming to answer its question. "This is just where I found myself when the light last shifted in my favor." I am beginning to understand that it is being coy, playful, not enigmatic. I wonder if it has been craving companionship like myself—so deeply the ache was easier to ignore than admit. So deeply we thought it easier to pursue the less impossible goal of exploring infinite worlds to complete ourselves.

"I haven't been here before," I say, then frown. When we arrived, I had no sensation of adding to myself, of taking one more miniscule step closer to wholeness. My companion wraps a sinuous limb across my shoulders.

"You uncovered a hidden self already in your possession," it says, and I find I don't question how it already knows my thoughts so well. It has brought me closer to completion than all the versions of myself I've so far collected. So why shouldn't it know my thoughts? But for all the serenity its presence provides, I am still plagued by a nebulous yearning.

"I want to see the reality you come from," I say, although we have spent barely any time taking in this glorious gilded town with its sparkling streets and towering trees.

It smiles, showing four rows of perfect blunt teeth. "Then we have much farther to go. What do you call yourself?"

I stop mid-stride, and it pulls me off the main thoroughfare so I am not an obstruction. Such a simple question has laid bare the cause of my longing, the absent piece that even this being's presence has not been able to replace or render insignificant.

"I...don't know," I say, and now the words are true. I cannot remember when I last called myself anything. The individual names of my collected selves do not apply to the more complete me created by their unity.

I have been alone so long I have not needed a name.

"It is another thing you already possess but have yet to discover," it says, as if it can sense me teetering on the edge—of what, I cannot say, but something that would obliterate me. "It will come to you in time." It pauses and I nod, but I am distant from it and this town of kings.

"You can call me Ifnar," it says.

Its name wipes away my perceptions; its vast deck splays out again for a disorienting moment before collapsing once more. In that instant I see how its name could not be anything but Ifnar.

"Let me show you my home." It takes my hand and weaves through the town with deft familiarity. As we move to the outskirts, we abandon our expectations, and my own meager collection of selves fans out. It is hard to look at Ifnar this way, hard for my mind to wrap around the vastness of its being. But to see it as any less seems disrespectful, a denial of all it has accomplished.

We are following Ifnar's own path back to where it started—once the gates open, they stay open, and we travelers all leave distinct trails as we pass through, like comets dragging tails behind. Maybe the paths fade if left untraversed; I have never ventured this far from mine. Will I be able to find my way back home? Will it matter if I can't? My heart beats a furious rhythm against my chest as my panic rises. *Just wipe it away*, I tell myself. *It's a perception, nothing more, don't let it take over wipe it away wipe it away wipe it away.* But before it can consume me, Ifnar pulls me through another portal, and I am awestruck.

It is a world only in the vaguest sense, and we at the barest beginning of life. I inhabit the collection of particles and microbes that in millennia will be me in this reality. Finding a new version of myself is like coming up for air after nearly drowning—a great relieving breath that burns and tingles through my whole self. A return to a normal function I hadn't realized was lacking until it resumed.

The environment around the miscellaneous particles that are Ifnar and myself is volcanic, riotous. Its power is more blatant than anywhere else I've explored. The incredible heat melts most of what it touches but forges what survives into something stronger, more resilient.

This is how Ifnar and I proceed. We follow its trail across numerous worlds, some familiar to me but most new. The length of our stay on each is determined only by our interest. During our travels, sometimes we talk about other beings we've encountered, what lighting allows us to see the gateways, or the most interesting places we've visited. But often we are silent. As I collect more of myself, as we make our way closer to Ifnar's home, my missing name haunts me.

I've been trying to let it come to me, opening my mind and hoping something in our travels will reveal it at last. But its absence has its own gravity that pulls me further and further from Ifnar and into an orbit of despair.

"Please stop," I beg as we reach a chilly reality composed mostly of a tempestuous liquid, in which we reside; it flows through us as it does around us—we are just shy of insubstantial.

"I still don't know my name," I say. In this body's odd language, it is a combination of elaborate tentacle movements and intricate bubbles.

"We are almost done." Once more Ifnar is so natural in this form, on this world. Everywhere we've visited has been its home. Is that what comes with a name? The idea of belonging anywhere? The sense of being complete even in incompleteness?

But I've been pulled too far into my new orbit. "I can't continue. I am a shadow; I am nothing. How can I journey with you when I am missing my most essential part?" But my numerous selves recoil at the thought of abandoning Ifnar. I may shatter apart if I leave it, lose everything that I have gained. But I can't proceed as I am either.

Ifnar does not seem surprised or upset. It weaves its gelatinous form around mine—an embrace that makes everything worse by being so comforting. I withdraw.

"How many sunsets have passed since we met?" it asks. At first I can't see what relevance this has to our parting ways. But as I try to count, try to track time in the only way that has meant anything to me, I realize I can't remember. Being with Ifnar has been more vital to my existence than the gates.

"Isn't my name important? More important than this?" I regret my hostile tone.

"It is, but it is not a requirement for this." Ifnar motions between us. "It will come in its own time, as we found each other by happenstance. It will come when you are ready to know. There is no point delaying everything else in the meantime."

"How can you know that? You already have your name! You have everything, belong anywhere." Because we are made of liquid, I cannot cry, but I wish I could. How can Ifnar understand the sucking emptiness of my missing name? I'm not sure I understand it myself—in the same way I struggle to take in the actuality of Ifnar, I have to impose perceptions to process the gap in my being. It is a negative space, an absence suggested only by the presence of surrounding pieces.

After a long silence, Ifnar replies. "I know because I did not always have my name." There is a sadness in its voice as deep as the liquid in which we exist. "And I recall that feeling." The echo of its pain reverberates in its words and silences me. All this while, I failed to imagine Ifnar any way other than in its current impressive state. But we all start as solitary fragments of a larger whole.

"I cannot ask you to keep going if you wish to stop," Ifnar continues. "But I ask that you follow me just once more. To my home."

This is the first time Ifnar has asked anything of me on our whole journey, though I have asked so much of it. I have sought so many answers, so much comfort, and have not had to reciprocate.

"Of course," I say, and this time I am the one embracing it. I can feel its sadness ebb, like a tide pulled by a moon's gravity. We float that way for a bit, intertwined. Then, tentacles clasped, Ifnar pulls me through our final portal.

I am standing on solid ground. Green grass. Blue sky. Birds singing. In the distance, buildings reach into the clouds. But this can't be right.

I look down at myself, at a too-familiar form. Two hands. Ten fingers. Two legs. This can't be right.

"But..." I say, looking up. Ifnar is similar in form, although its skin is a beautiful onyx to my tawny brown. "...this is my home."

Ifnar nods. "Mine as well."

And I don't know what's different about being home this time, but it's as if all the liquid from the previous reality is still within me, rushing to fill that negative space. In an instant I am free from the orbit of despair, knocked clear by new knowledge. I know my name, and I can hardly believe it had eluded me for so long.

"Entne," I say, and again I am a conduit, all my selves vibrating through spacetime in unison with this insight. I could shake the universe apart if I chose.

Ifnar smiles, then takes my hand. "Now you too have everything."